They stood together in the north-west tower, looking out at the lands of World's Edge, its forest and hills, its ruined cities.

The enchantments that overlaid the land weren't visible to the ordinary senses, but they were nevertheless real. Curses and spells and hauntings sat upon the earth like a miasma of decay. The land was dying.

"Look," said Sirion Hilversun softly. "Here we stand by the world's very edge, forgotten people in a forgotten land. To the east is the great cliff, and chaos.... To the west there are whole continents free from the terrors and uncertainties that haunt our land..."

"It wasn't like that once," Helen said, interrupting him.

The enchanter smiled. "Perhaps," he said. "But that was before either of us were born. You and I came to a world that was already lost, already wrecked by wars of enchantment.... I should have sent you away years ago."

"No!" she said sharply. She repeated it in a softer tone, almost a pleading tone. "No."

Brian Stableford

The Last Days
of the
Edge
of the
World

ACE FANTASY BOOKS
NEW YORK

This Ace Book contains the complete
text of the original hardcover edition.
It has been completely reset in a typeface
designed for easy reading, and was printed
from new film.

THE LAST DAYS OF THE EDGE OF THE WORLD

An Ace Fantasy Book / published by arrangement with
the author

PRINTING HISTORY
Hutchinson edition published 1978
Ace edition / September 1985

ISBN: 0-441-47077-7

Ace Fantasy Books are published by The Berkley Publishing Group,
200 Madison Avenue, New York, New York 10016.
PRINTED IN THE UNITED STATES OF AMERICA

For Ken and Jo Wild

SIRION HILVERSUN WAS waiting for a letter. He was not sure exactly when it would arrive, but he remembered that it would be in the near future. The waiting bothered him, because his memory was so bad these days that he would have to wait until the letter arrived before he could find out what was in it.

Sirion Hilversun was, by birth and by profession, a man of magical means—an enchanter. But he was also very old, and magic does not stand up well to the ravages of time. In his youth he had been able to remember quite clearly all of his past and quite a considerable fraction of his future: in those days he had always known when he was. Nowadays he lived in the midst of an awful turmoil of yesterday and tomorrow. His daughter Helen, who kept the calendar and had the only unmagical (and therefore trustworthy) clock in Moonmansion, always had to remind him which slice of his life he was actually in the process of living.

Moonmansion was Sirion Hilversun's home. It was very large, having to accommodate the customary complement of secret passages and hidden chambers as well as the more mundane facilities. It resembled a castle, with great grey towers and neat battlements, but that was just for show. No army had ever occupied the mansion, and none had laid siege to it. All the *real* castles in the lands of the World's Edge had been reduced to ruins in the wars of enchantment over two centuries before.

While Sirion Hilversun waited for the mysterious letter he paced the battlements, trying desperately to sort out what was what (or possibly when was when). Today was Tuesday, and the letter had arrived—was to arrive—on a Tuesday. It could hardly be last Tuesday, but it might be next Tuesday, although the memory seemed too fresh. These days, whenever he remembered something as if it were yesterday, it was almost always today—or, in extreme cases, tomorrow.

He shook his head, wishing that time had been organized in a simpler fashion. It seemed so complicated that he wondered how people with ordinary one-way memories managed at all. How could they ever keep their appointments?

Every time the enchanter reached the limit of the line he was pacing he paused momentarily to stare out over the sprawling lands of the World's Edge. They were still deep-laden with enchantment, most of which was the legacy of the great wars. In some places there were curses and counter-curses stacked six or seven deep, and the overcrowding of ghosts in some of the older ruins was positively awful. These were the last lands on Earth where magic still ruled, and this was the last of the Old World's seven edges. All the rest had been claimed by science, reason and roundness. Sometimes, Sirion Hilversun wondered how this last little enclave could possibly survive, and always came to the conclusion that, in the long run, it would not. The tide of time was against it. He was reasonably sure that he would not see the day that magic died (although he couldn't remember, and might be quite wrong), but he did worry about Helen. She hadn't much magic, but she relied a lot on what she had, and she loved these lands very deeply.

While he paused slightly longer than usual, his legs tiring somewhat, though his eyes still searched the roads and hillsides for a rider with a mailbag, Helen came out from the north-west tower in search of him.

"It's time for lunch," she told him.

"Lunch?" he repeated. The word couldn't quite penetrate his fog of thought, and he turned it over in his mind as if it were something strange—a sound devoid of meaning.

"You know," she said. "Food. Sandwiches. Cups of tea. Things to eat."

The last word broke through.

"Eat!" he said. "I can't eat! Important events are about to get under way. There's important news winging its way here right now. I *know* it's important, though I can't for the life of me remember what it is. Terribly important."

"Impatience won't help," Helen pointed out. "Pacing up and down will only make your feet sore. These battlements are cold. And I've told you before about those silly slippers with the curled-up toes. If the wind changes you'll get rheumatism again."

"I've got a spell to cure rheumatism," muttered the enchanter. "And these slippers are very fashionable."

"The letter will come just as quickly if you wait inside," said Helen firmly.

Sirion Hilversun looked at his daughter, trying to muster a stern paternal frown. He couldn't manage it. He sighed.

He allowed Helen to lead him down into the heart of Moonmansion, by winding stairs and twisting corridors. It always seemed that one had to go a long way to achieve a short distance. He often wondered—especially when he got lost—whether the gnomes who had built the place had followed his blueprints properly.

When they finally reached the dining room Sirion Hilversun all but collapsed into his chair.

"Watch your elbows," complained the chair. "Where d'y'wannago?"

"Nowhere," said Sirion Hilversun. "I just want to eat my lunch."

"Aw," said the chair, "you're no fun any more. What's the point of having a wishing chair if all you do is sit on it to eat your lunch? You haven't taken me out in a year. I have feelings, you know. I've a good mind to go on strike."

"You can't," said the enchanter. "That's the clock's job. Or it was until I mislaid his chimes."

"Never mind talking to your chair," said Helen. "Eat your lunch."

The enchanter sighed. Helen had a distinctly down-to-earth attitude to life. It was not surprising in one so young, especially one so young who had only a one-way memory. But sometimes he wished that she had just a *little* more magic about her. It was not the fact that she could only conjure little things that worried him so much as the fact that she couldn't see the future *at all*. It gave her the wrong attitude to life. No foresight.

He ate his lunch, slowly and carefully. He forgot what he had eaten while he was still in the middle of it.

Meanwhile, in the city of Jessamy, the capital of the utterly unmagical land of Caramorn, there was something of a crisis. Owing to a geographical accident Caramorn was the unmagical nation that lay closest to the lands of World's Edge. In the not-too-distant past Caramorn had actually been a land where magic was welcome, but nearly a hundred and fifty years before the great king Rufus Malagig I had published a royal decree banishing it from the land. Ever since that day the fortunes of Caramorn had been on the wane. The once-rich kingdom had become steadily poorer, until by now the nation had passed through all the many stages of mediocrity and was, not to put too fine a point on it, at rock bottom. The present king, Rufus Malagig IV, was in conference with his ministers, facing utter and ultimate ruin.

"Basically," said Alcover, "we're bankrupt." Alcover was the chancellor of the exchequer—a small, wizened man with a wonderful head for figures. He looked very unhappy, mostly because the figure that was occupying his wonderful head right now was a zero of positively horrific proportions.

"That's impossible," said the king, a tall, imposing man with a perpetual expression of wide-eyed innocence. He had inherited from his auspicious forefathers a habit of saying "That's impossible" whenever he was faced with a serious problem, confident that it would thus disappear. Lately, however, he had discovered that the limits of possibility are not determined by royal decree.

"Your majesty has his own key to the treasury," murmured Alcover patiently. "Take a look. If your majesty can find a single brass farthing, he is most welcome to it. It will represent the entire extent of the kingdom's riches."

Rufus Malagig IV stared into space for a few moments, contemplating the awful idea of poverty. He couldn't quite believe it. He was a *king*, and kings were never, ever poor.

"Well," he said, "it's up to you chaps to do something about it. That's what ministers are for. That's what I pay you for."

The prime minister, Coronado—a long, lean man with a lantern jaw—coughed politely. "At the moment," he commented, "your majesty isn't exactly paying us at all. But the point is that there's nothing more we can do. We have, so to speak, shot our last bolt."

"Collect a tax!" said Rufus, with an airy wave of the hand. "That's what my father always did. Make the public pay!"

The home secretary, whose name was Hallowbrand, leaned forward. The chair on which he sat creaked under the strain: a great deal of weight had to be redistributed when Hallowbrand changed his position. "The simple fact, sire," he said, "is that the public *can't* pay. They haven't got any money either. This is the third year running the harvest has been poor, and for the last thirty years we've known that two or three years without a wheat surplus would see us over the edge...."

"The money must be *somewhere*," the king interrupted, rudely. "It can't just have disappeared into thin air."

"It has all gone to pay moneylenders and merchants," said Alcover, gently. *"Foreign* moneylenders and merchants. Even when the harvest is bad the people have to eat. We have to import what we need... and we have to pay for what we import. All the gold in Caramorn—

all the gold that *was* in Caramorn—is in the Western Empire now, mostly in Heliopolis. When I say that we are bankrupt I mean that the whole *kingdom* is bankrupt. The situation is so desperate that if we don't pay the wages of the palace guard soon there is a definite danger that they might walk out, or even turn against us . . . in which case certain unruly elements in the populace would almost certainly . . ."

The king stared at him. The chancellor trailed off, leaving the rest to the royal imagination.

"A *revolution?*" whispered the king.

"I fear," said Hallowbrand, "that it's a possibility."

"But my people *love* me," protested Rufus. "I'm a *good* king. It's not my fault we've had bad harvests."

"Actually," said Coronado, "you aren't such a bad king, as kings go. But when times are bad it's the king that tends to take the blame, whether he deserves it or not. It's an old saying—the crown carries the can."

"Oh," said the king. Then he lapsed into silence. He could think of nothing more to say.

"We have already begun what might be termed emergency measures," said Alcover, trying to break it as gently as possible. "We're selling the silver, and the horses. We would have had to sell the queen's jewellery, except that when we approached her majesty we learned that it had gone to Heliopolis already—a private deal, if you know what I mean. The very last thing which is of any real value is the library. The university at Heliopolis is very interested in it because it contains a lot of material relating to magic and the like—biographies of the enchanters, histories of haunting, things like that. A local boy who is studying at the university has come home to catalogue it."

"The silver!" said the king, faintly. "My horses! Even

the library! I can keep my crown, I hope?"

"That," grunted Bellegrande, "is the object of the exercise." Bellegrande wore a perpetual expression of great sadness and was much given to bitter comments. He was, however, very good at languages.

"The thing is," said Alcover, "even this won't be enough. It will keep us going until next spring, but even if there's a bumper harvest we'll still have our backs to the wall. We're done for unless we can find something else to turn the tide in our favor."

"What do you suggest?" said the king, acidly. "Inviting the enchanters back?"

There fell upon the conference table a deep and profound silence. The king looked at each of his ministers in turn. They each looked back, with faces that seemed to be carved from stone.

"Oh dear," said the king, weakly realizing what the silence meant. "You *do* want me to invite the enchanters back."

The king was rather nervous of magic. The thought of wizardry and curses and hauntings and the like had always frightened him rather more than somewhat.

"We've thought it over carefully," said Coronado, "and we think there's one chance. Not a day's ride from here is the home of Sirion Hilversun, a place called Moonmansion. He was one of the enchanters banished by your great-grandfather, but prior to that banishment they were friends. I don't think the enchanter took it too hard—I think he understood King Rufus I's reasons. But the point is that he has a daughter—a very young daughter. By all accounts the lands of magic aren't what they used to be, and it may be that Sirion Hilversun *could* be persuaded to return, under the right circumstances, and the right circumstances might involve making a reasonable marriage for his daughter. Do you see what I mean, sire?"

King Rufus Malagig IV bounded to his feet and thumped the table. "Of course I see what you mean, you loathsome toad!" he bellowed. "You want to marry Prince Damian off to a witch!"

"Please calm down, sire," urged Coronado. "We must try to be sensible and level-headed about this. I assure you that the girl doesn't have green scales or purple wings or warts, or even a black cat and broomstick. She's very beautiful, and it's rumoured that she has very little magical talent—which is another reason why Sirion Hilversun might think it a good idea to find her a secure place in the Western World. I'm afraid, sire, that things being as they are you don't have a lot of choice. Prince Damian is the only asset we have left—the kingdom's only hope. If he doesn't make this marriage, he might not be a prince much longer . . . and you might not be a king."

Hallowbrand drew from the vast pocket of his cloak a letter, already sealed. "We have taken the liberty, sire," he said, ponderously, "of preparing the proposal. If you will give your approval now, I will send it at once."

The king looked down at his seated ministers. They were all so calm and so deadly serious. The rage ebbed out of him, and his face went quite grey.

"Is it *really* the only way?" he whispered.

"The only way," intoned Coronado.

"Have you told Damian?"

The prime minister shook his head. "We thought . . . a job for his father."

"Oh," said the king. He sagged rather than sat back down into his chair. "Oh, of course." His eyes fell, until he was staring down at the bare table-top. "It's impossible," he murmured.

Then he remembered who he was, and he looked up again.

"For the good of the kingdom," he said, sternly. "Send it."

"I won't do it," said Helen, firmly.

Sirion Hilversun peered at her over the rims of his bifocals. His expression was very serious.

"It's a very polite letter," he said. "And I don't see why it's such a terrible idea. Most girls would be quite attracted to the idea of marrying a prince."

"I'm not most girls," she said.

"No," murmured the enchanter, "you aren't."

There was a long pause. They stood together in the north-west tower, looking out of the windows at the lands of World's Edge—its forests and its hills, its valleys and streams, its ruined cities and sunken roads.

The enchantments that overlaid the land weren't really visible to the ordinary senses, but they were nevertheless real, and no one with a hint of magic in his (or her) eye could possibly be ignorant of them. Curses and spells

11

and hauntings sat upon the good earth like a miasma of decay. Moonmansion was a tiny haven in a world of dark coverts and corners, shadows from another existence. The land was dying, although it was frozen in time. There was little that was good and bright out there now.

In the far west the sun was sinking towards the towers of Heliopolis, which lay beyond the horizon. It would still be lighting the cities of the New World, standing high above the Western Empire, bright and beautiful in a coach of fine, white clouds.

"Look," said Sirion Hilversun, softly. "Here we stand by the world's very edge, forgotten people in a forgotten land. To the east there is the great cliff, and chaos . . . a grey emptiness that walls us in. To the west there are whole continents free from all the terrors and uncertainties that haunt our land. . . ."

"It wasn't like that once," said Helen, interrupting him.

The enchanter smiled. "Perhaps," he said. "But that was before either of us were born. You and I came into a world that was already lost, already wrecked by the wars of enchantment. It's the only world you and I have ever known. It's the only magical world there is, now. Perhaps, once, there was a Golden Age . . . but when you get to my age you'll wonder. To me, it doesn't matter. I've lived my life as I chose. But for you, I think there has to be something better. Something brighter."

"But don't you see," said Helen, "your kind of life is the kind of life *I* want to live. It's what *I* choose. I love Moonmansion. I want to stay here."

"But it's all you've ever known," said Sirion Hilversun. "How can you know?"

Helen looked out of the window. She leaned over the sill, looking out towards Methwold forest, searching the deepening evening for the shadows of the forgotten city of Ora Lamae. *There,* it was true, was decay and desolation. It was not a pleasant place. Nor, for that matter, was Methwold itself, which was dark green from without and black and dry within. Such places no longer existed in the Western World, save as myths and legends and the stuff of nightmares. She couldn't honestly say that she liked them, but she was used to them. She knew them. They were *real*.

"I don't want to go away," she whispered.

"You owe it to yourself," said Sirion Hilversun. "You must look beyond these horizons. Perhaps, as you seem to believe, the Western World is not what people claim. But you must go to *see*. You can't just stay here and reject it out of hand. You're young. All this is bad for you. . . . I should have sent you away years ago."

"No!" she said, sharply. Then, knowing that he meant well, that he was sincere in everything he said, she repeated it in a softer tone, almost a pleading tone: "No."

The enchanter looked down again at the letter in his hand, reading it for the fortieth time, though he had not forgotten its contents.

"I don't want to marry," said Helen. "Not a prince, not anyone. I don't believe that life is just a matter of attaching oneself to a man——the most highly placed man available——and then drifting along in his wake. I'd rather make my own way in the world, in command of my own life."

"It's not that easy," said the enchanter. "Not even with magic to help."

"You're always so very sure that nothing's easy," she said. "The trouble with you is that you won't try. You give up and let things go the way they are. You have magical power and skill and knowledge. Perhaps if you were willing to try we could do something here in the magic lands. We could fight the decay, give the land some of its life again. If you weren't always so determined to let events flow over and around you we might not be *trapped* the way we are."

She seemed very close to tears. Sirion Hilversun didn't know what to say. She turned away from the window and from him, looking through moist eyes at the ancient furniture which crammed the room: magic carpets eaten away by magic moths, tables with broken legs, clocks with broken hearts, cracked crystal balls and magic mirrors which had long ago turned in upon their own reflections. He watched her stir at the dust which overlaid a gryphon-skin rug with her slipper.

"The powers I have are no match for those that made our world what it is," said the enchanter meekly. "Only Jeahawn the Judge could begin to sort things out after the war, and he could do no more than put all the released forces under check. He couldn't undo the damage which had been done—that would have taken more than a hundred years, and the most powerful spell ever written. There's none alive now who could ever make such a spell. The decay will have to run its course, and in all likelihood these lands will be sick for ever and ever."

"I know," she said. "You remember it all as if it were tomorrow. There's no hope. What will be will be."

Now he was close to tears, too. She realized this, and relented.

"I don't mean to be unkind," she said. "I'm sorry. I really am. But you don't realize how much you're asking of me. What's this prince like? I might not like him. Why is the king of Caramorn suddenly offering me his son anyhow? It's been three generations since a king of Caramorn last talked to you, and that was to tell you to get out of his kingdom or else."

"He didn't put it quite like that," said Sirion Hilversun, trying hard to remember. "He was decent enough, as kings go. It wasn't his idea, really, though he had no love for magic in himself. It was popular demand. The peasants were always prejudiced against us—too many hedgewizards and charlatans making a pest of themselves, I suppose. I dare say the common people never got much joy out of magic—none that they could count in their wallets. And they were always afraid. Rufus made himself very popular by expelling us all, as I remember it. He always did want to be remembered as a king the people loved."

"All right, then," said Helen. "So why is his great-grandson trying to re-import magic into the realm?"

The enchanter shrugged. It didn't seem to him to be a very important question. The important question was how to persuade Helen that this really was all for the best.

"I'm going to invite the king, and the prince, and his ministers over for a banquet," declared the enchanter. "It's the only thing to do. You can see Damian and he can see you. And if all is satisfactory arrangements can commence. That's what we'll do. And it will all come out right.... Just you see if it doesn't."

Helen shook her head, but decided that it was wiser to say no more. Time would tell. There was no harm in having a look at the prince. And then...

Well, she would think of something.

"You have *got* to be joking," said Damian to his father. It was not a wise remark. King Rufus Malagig IV was not in a good temper, and the crown prince always seemed to bring out the worst in his temper, even when it was at its best.

"This is *no joke*," said the king, through gritted teeth.

"The future of the kingdom depends on this. My future. Your future. Just for once you are going to do as you are told and you are going to do it *right*."

"I don't want to marry a witch," said Damian. "I'd rather marry a kitchen-maid than some horrible hag with magical powers. I don't care if we are bankrupt. I've been bankrupt for years, since you cut off my allowance. I'm used to it. Furthermore, dear father..."

"Shut up!" roared the king.

A group of starlings sitting on the palace roof took flight in panic, although the king and the prince were in the throne room three floors down. Rufus Malagig had often been complimented on the magnitude of the royal roar.

Damian sniffed. "There's no need to be like that about it," he said. Although he was a rather sickly youth, and puny to boot, he had long since given up cowering before his father. He had grown used to the roar over the years, and he knew that the king was too soft of heart to back it up with any real action. Damian had long since learned that endurance was all that was required to win family arguments in the court of Caramorn.

"If your majesty pleases," said Coronado, who was standing to one side, "perhaps I could explain to the prince the reasons of state which make this marriage necessary."

"Never mind the reasons of state," snorted the king. "It's not his place to demand explanations. He'll do as he's told."

"I will not," said the prince, with an air of martyred innocence. "And it ill becomes you to suggest that I should."

"She only has a *few* magical powers, dear," put in the queen, desperately trying to pour oil on the troubled waters.

"That," said Damian, "is like saying that she only has a few measles, or a slight case of the plague."

"Perhaps," interposed Coronado cunningly, "the young highness is afraid of magic."

"I am not!" said Damian. This was a lie, of a variety which he told often. His one passionate belief was that discretion was the better part of valour. He had never been known to say "boo" to a goose, or even to a larger-than-average duck.

"Oh, well," said Coronado slyly, "perhaps it's just women that he's afraid of."

"I am *not!*" repeated Damian, turning red and stamping his foot. Though he lacked the volume, he had obviously inherited something of his father's talent for bellowing.

"Ah," said Coronado, "such courage. And for the sake of his country, too. The people will love you for this, young sire."

Damian furrowed his brow, trying to remember whether anything had slipped out that shouldn't have. "Now wait a minute," he said. "I didn't say that..."

"It's not everyone," Coronado went on, "who would stand up forthrightly and say: 'If my country needs me, I shall not flinch. I am not afraid to do what has to be done.' You're not afraid, are you?"

"Well," said Damian, "no... but let's not rush into anything. I mean, we don't know anything about this girl, and... well, there may be perfectly good reasons."

"Oh, precisely, sire," said Coronado. "You take the words out of my mouth."

"Do I?" said Damian, by now hopelessly lost.

"And I couldn't agree more," Coronado hurried on. "Exactly as you say. We need to know more. And that is why we are all going to dine at the enchanter's home tomorrow evening. Then we can, as you have so shrewdly observed, find out more about the girl, and whether she is really *worthy* to marry your august self."

"Oh," said the prince, slowly. "Yes, well . . . I'm glad you see it my way. Sensible, that. We'll go check up on them. But I warn you, I'm very suspicious of this whole affair. Very suspicious indeed. It's not that I'm afraid . . . not in the least. Not of anything. But one has to be *cautious*, you see. Very cautious."

Still trying to figure out exactly where the conversation had taken him, the prince left the room.

Coronado and the king exchanged troubled glances.

"He's not going to co-operate," said the king.

"The thing *I* worry about," said Coronado, "is whether *she*'ll co-operate once she's clapped eyes on him."

"What a terrible thing to say," complained the queen. "Is that any way to talk about the prince? Rufus? Are you going to let him talk about our son that way?"

"He *is* a prince," pointed out Rufus Malagig IV. "She can't expect everything. And he's not *that* bad."

"Oh!" said the queen. "You're just as bad as he is. Your own son! Not content with bartering him in marriage to a wizard, you have to insult him as well. How *could* you!"

And, with that, the queen stormed out.

The king shifted uneasily on the throne. He took off his crown and looked at it thoughtfully, then dusted off a mark with his shirt cuff. He gave Coronado a rueful glance.

"Are you *sure* this is the only way?" he asked.

"The only way," confirmed the prime minister dourly.

"It's not going to be easy."

"True," sighed Coronado. "Very true."

He wondered, idly, about the possibilities that might be open to an experienced administrator and diplomat in

Heliopolis. But he was too old to start working his way up from the bottom again——or even from the middle.

"Well," said the king, "I only hope it's a good banquet. It might be our last."

HELEN STOOD IN front of one of the few magic mirrors in Moonmansion that was still in any kind of working order. She had claimed it for her bedroom on the grounds that her need was greater than her father's.

"Mirror, mirror on the wall," she recited, "who is the fairest of us all?"

"Vanity," said the mirror, in tones of mild reproof, "is *not nice*."

"You can't get out of it like that," said Helen. "You have to answer the question. It's in your contract."

"It's a *silly* question," said the mirror. "All of who? Or do I mean whom? And what do you mean by 'fairest'? If I'm contractually bound to answer questions, then it stands to reason that you must put questions which are answerable."

"Oh, all right," she said, tiredly. "Dc I look all right?"

"What do you mean by . . . ?" the mirror began, but then relented as the expression on Helen's face began to change. "Don't look like that," it said. "You might crack me. You look fine. Quite lovely."

Helen smiled, and the mirror relaxed. It always felt good when it reflected a nice smile.

There was a knock on the door and Sirion Hilversun hurried in. He was dressed in his best robes—purple ones with a neat dressing of stars around the cuffs and the hem, gathered at the waist by a silver girdle.

"The prince and his party are just coming over the hill," he said. "Are you ready?"

"Of course," replied Helen, trying to suggest total boredom in the way that she spoke. She made some small adjustment to the placement of her hairpins.

"Then come on, come on. . . . We haven't got all day."

Helen refused to be hurried. In the ancient romances princesses *never* hurried. She was concentrating hard on being genteel and dignified.

In the two days which had elapsed since the idea of marrying a prince had been introduced to her she had relented slightly in her opposition to it. She had re-read a couple of the old romances, which made marrying princes seem like quite a good idea. If this Prince Damian was all that princes were supposed to be, then there might be a certain attraction in the possibility. Also, of course, her father did so desperately want this marriage to take place, and the last thing in the world that she wanted was to hurt him.

So she followed her father downstairs to the great banquet hall with feelings that were more than a little mixed. She was, if the truth be known, very apprehensive of the occasion. No one ever came to Moonmansion these days, and she had not been accustomed to seeing people since she was very small. She was used to conversation with magical devices and all manner of creatures, and had even passed the time of day with friendly ghosts on occasion, but real people was something she had not run across in some years.

Moonmansion did not look at all its usual lazy, dusty self. It had been well and truly cleaned up and tidied, and appeared positively radiant with magical magnificence. All the cabinets full of treasure-trove trinkets which had accumulated in the attics had been hauled out, because Sirion Hilversun seemed to recall that unmagical men were very impressed by such things. Because there weren't enough suits of armour to fill up every alcove a couple of green porcelain dragons had been brought in from the laundry room, where their outstretched arms (they were dragons rampant) were normally used to hang wet washing.

Personally, Helen thought it a little unfortunate that her father had not thought it necessary to remove the seventy-seven chiming clocks from the walls of the great hall, but at least she had dissuaded him from winding them up.

There were servants everywhere. In the normal course of affairs Helen, with the aid of a few magic spells and wonderful devices provided by her father, did most of the housework herself, and the rest went largely undone. For the special occasion, however, Sirion Hilversun had thought it polite to put on a show, and thus had rooted out an old spell for turning mice into footmen, which he had picked up cheap at an auction in his youth. Helen hadn't really thought that it would work, but it had apparently been the property of a fairy godmother of the highest repute. Although it had a strict time clause in the small print the spell actually went off a treat.

While the enchanter and his daughter, resplendent in their most extravagant clothes, stood in the midst of all this grandeur at the foot of the stairway, two of the exmice opened the front door. One especially handsome mouse took up a position beside the best suit of armour and began announcing the guests by name. He did a first-rate job, not misplacing a single syllable.

The foreign minister and his wife led the royal party, followed by the other ministers. The king, queen and prince brought up the rear. The ministers and their wives stood to either side, forming a kind of corridor along which the royal family could advance to meet their hosts. When the whole party had been properly presented and introduced, their own servants—not one of whom was, or ever had been, a mouse—were admitted.

The big moment, of course, was the introduction of the young couple. As they were urged towards one another by their respective fathers, they exchanged long, suspicious stares.

Prince Damian should, logically, have been most impressed. Helen was a beautiful girl, although perhaps not cast in the mould of the princesses of ancient romance. She was, perhaps, a little tall and a little more *healthy* than those delicate and precious creatures. Her hair was cut short and her posture was aggressive rather than demure. But none of these things detracted from her beauty—and, indeed, were part and parcel of it. Nevertheless, despite it all, Damian was not overcome. He found her rather intimidating, even before he took into account any supernatural abilities. While not exactly quivering in his shoes, he was more than a little apprehensive both of her and the surroundings. His greeting was lukewarm, to say the least.

Helen had a little more excuse for her lack of enthusiasm. Even carefully dressed up, the prince seemed undersized and sallow of complexion. His features were not exactly unhandsome, but their aspect was ruined by the expression which he wore—a mixture of vanity and nervousness, with a slight hint of slyness. Helen was not impressed. Not at all.

The encounter—indeed, the whole banquet to which it was a prelude—was something of a failure. It never really got under way. The food was excellent, but the guests did not quite trust it. They were all too well aware that the Arts Magical had been involved in its preparation. In Caramorn, the Arts Magical was definitely one of those subjects not suitable for discussion in mixed company. Unfortunately, the mixed company in Moonmansion on this occasion could discover few topics of conversation which did not touch upon them, and for this reason a certain awkwardness preyed upon all of the table talk.

It was not long before virtually everyone was looking forward expectantly to the time when the guests could tactfully take themselves back to Jessamy. They had prudently decided not to spend the night in the magic lands. Both Rufus Malagig IV and Sirion Hilversun tried hard to inject some real *bonhomie* into the occasion, but the atmosphere defeated even the diplomatic talents of Coronado. Helen and Damian exchanged contemplative glances over the soup, but by the time the main course arrived they had each decided that the whole idea was unworthy of serious thought. Each, independently, settled on a policy of ignoring the other. They both became very quiet and resistant to questions addressed to them from elsewhere, retreating into invisible shells from whence it was impossible to coax them. Even when the time came for the farewells and *au revoirs* they stood apart.

The enchanter and the king exchanged expressions of

hearty good fellowship and wished one another well. Tactfully, they avoided any overt reference to the marriage or the likelihood of any formal engagement. Then they parted, each to apply himself to his own part of the problem.

When all the guests had gone, and the footmen had turned back into mice, while candles cast a dim light over the banqueting table and left the suits of armour and porcelain dragons to the gloomy shadows, Sirion Hilversun and his daughter sat together, sadly and apprehensively. They were both full of food, and neither wanted an argument. Helen's anger and resentment were at a low ebb.

"I know he's not the sort of prince you find in story books," said the enchanter, "but few real princes are. But he'll grow a little yet, and with a little encouragement."

"I don't want to marry him," said Helen flatly.

"He *is* a prince," said the enchanter.

"I'd rather marry a swineherd. What's so important about princes?"

"You don't know," said Sirion Hilversun, in a low voice. "You don't understand." To him, it was important . . . as important as anything could be. He wanted to die knowing that his daughter was secure, and the greatest security there could be—the greatest security he could imagine—was that of being married to the heir to a throne. He had always wanted the best for Helen, and a prince, by definition, *was* the best. Had he known about the grievous state of Caramorn's economy, his attitude would have been different. But he didn't. And neither did Helen.

Helen looked hard at her father, who was looking just now as old and as feeble as he had *ever* looked. She knew as well as he did that the fading of his remarkable memory and the fading of his magical powers were the inevitable preludes to his death. She accepted that as he did. And she wanted very much to ease his mind. She knew that the only way to do it was to give in to his stubbornness—but she also knew that there was no way on Earth that she was going to marry Damian of Caramorn.

She hunted in her mind for a way out of the dilemma.

All of a sudden she remembered something she had read long before, in one of the romances of which she was so fond.

"Father," she said, trying to sound perfectly calm and sensible. "I'll marry your prince on one condition. If he can prove that he's not a fool by answering three questions that I will put to him, then I'll marry him."

Sirion Hilversun stared at her thoughtfully. He had read that story too. The young lady in question had never intended to marry at all, and she had asked questions which she considered to be unanswerable. He could see Helen's strategy quite clearly. But the enchanter also remembered the end of the story, when a prince had come who *could* answer the questions. And that romance had ended happily. He hesitated, wondering what to say.

"That's very unusual," he said.

"It's been done before," answered Helen, reasonably. "And you wouldn't want me to marry a worthless prince, now would you? You'd want me to marry one with a little common sense, a little cleverness, and perhaps a little initiative. If Prince Damian hasn't any of those qualities he'd be a most unsuitable husband. I'm sure you'll agree with that."

"Perhaps," said the enchanter, slowly. "Perhaps."

"I think you should write a letter first thing tomorrow morning," urged Helen.

"I can't help thinking," said the enchanter, "that it's

a little unfair. After all, the prince is a prince and you're the daughter of a fairly mediocre magician. He might feel very insulted by such a demand."

"Fair enough," replied Helen, thinking quickly. "You can tell him that the offer applies both ways. If he'll prove himself by answering my questions. I'll prove myself by answering his. Three each. Who could object to that?"

Sirion Hilversun gave a low laugh. "I suppose you intend to play this game fairly," he said. "No daughter of mine would think to cheat by failing to answer a question that was put to her, and thus break the marriage contract."

"How could you suggest such a thing?" asked Helen, with an attitude of outrage that was almost wholly genuine. "When I play a game I play it by the rules. Believe you me, if that weakling prince can answer my questions, I'll answer his. No one's ever going to say that *I* was unworthy to marry a creature like *that*. I have my pride, you know."

"I know," murmured Sirion Hilversun. "I know."

The more he thought about it, the more the enchanter saw the suggestion as a way out—one way that perhaps *everyone* could be happy. If Damian really could answer the questions, and test Helen with some good ones of his own, then they might actually win one another's respect—something they had conspicuously failed to do earlier that evening.

There was, of course, a strong element of wishful thinking involved in Sirion Hilversun's contemplation. He still had certain illusions about the nature and talents of princes that owed more to stories and legends than any trustworthy experience. But it is always easy to believe when you desperately *want* to believe.

There was something more. While he thought about

the idea, a thin fragment of memory wound itself into his thoughts . . . something about questions and answers, and letters exchanged . . . something momentous. He couldn't remember anything specific, but he was suddenly seized by the notion that this suggestion was very important, and that on this decision might hang more than he could suspect. Something in his mind said that this was the most important decision of his life, and that he must take it correctly.

A shiver ran suddenly down his spine.

"What's the matter?" asked Helen, seeing the shudder.

"Magic," whispered Sirion Hilversun. "Powerful magic. I sense it."

"I don't know what you mean."

"Neither do I," said the enchanter. "It's beyond me. . . . Something from a long time ago. I want you to be careful, Helen. Very careful."

"Of course," she said. "Does that mean you agree?"

"I'll write the letter," said Sirion Hilversun. "Not in the morning. Right now, I'll put in your condition. But I want you to choose your questions carefully. Very carefully indeed."

"Oh, I will," she replied, with a slight hint of ironic triumph in her voice. "I will. You can depend on that."

"WHAT I WANT to know," said the king, furiously, "is what on Earth the fellow means by it. Silly nonsense about questions. What questions? Is he trying to suggest that Damian's a fool? I won't stand for it, I tell you!"

"It's definitely an insult," said Damian, feeding the flames of his father's rage. "After this, I'd say that there would be no point at all in carrying on with this plan. We still have our pride. The marriage is out of the question." He realized that he had accidentally made a pun and looked around to see if anyone had noticed. Nobody had. He shrugged philosophically. It was probably not the time for levity anyhow.

"Please," said Coronado, "let's take this calmly. I understand your point of view. But what we must understand is that World's Edge has customs and folkways that differ considerably from our own. The magic lands are steeped in ritual and superstition. Nothing is simple and straightforward where enchanters are concerned. All things have to be dressed in strange ceremony. I seem to remember reading somewhere about a custom very similar to this, and it is quite wonderful to think that such things are still being preserved. A man of Sirion Hilversun's antiquity, you must realize, is bound to be very strong on tradition. It isn't an insult. I think that we must, in all honour and with all dignity, accept."

The prime minister finished his speech with a small bow. Whenever he thought that he had made an especially fine speech he finished it thus. He was particularly proud of this one because he had done it, so to speak, off the cuff.

The king writhed on the throne. It was not a very comfortable throne, and he had often considered getting rid of it and replacing it with a nice armchair, but somehow the idea always seemed slightly absurd when he got to the point of being about to mention it to someone else, and he never did.

"I don't know," muttered the king. He had been impressed by Coronado's speech, but his rages always took a while to wear off.

"*I'm* not so sure that this is a good idea anyway," said Damian. "It seems to me we're taking a lot for granted. How do we know that his deal will do any of us any good. That old man looks pretty useless to me. I don't see how *he's* going to save the kingdom."

"If nothing else," put in Alcover, "he's got assets. Those porcelain dragons are worth more than a little, and that collection of clocks contains some priceless antiques. I calculate that to maintain the staff we saw last night and to keep a house the size of Moonmansion running smoothly he must have a budget of at least a thousand a week. That doesn't sound much, but when you consider that he has no income at all, and must be living on his capital, or the interest it earns. . . ."

"With all due respect to Alcover," said Bellegrande, "the enchanter's household budget is neither here nor there. What matters is his magic. And that he has in abundance. You may not have noticed, but I overheard some of those footmen in communication, and I assure you that they spoke no language I've ever heard before. It's my belief they're supernatural creatures enslaved by his enchantment. *That* is real power."

"He sets a very good table," rumbled Hallowbrand. "A man who sets a good table is a good man to have on your side. That's what I always say."

It did not take an intellectual giant to see which way the current of opinion was flowing. That was perhaps as well, as one thing Damian was not was an intellectual giant.

"Honestly!" complained the prince. "Anyone would think that the wizard had you all under a spell or something. You're all so keen to deliver me into his witch-daughter's clutches. No one cares what *I* think. And in any case, what makes you think I'll be able to answer her stupid questions?"

There was a slightly uncomfortable silence. The ministers exchanged significant glances. The last question was most definitely an awkward one.

"If I may make a suggestion . . ." said Hallowbrand tentatively.

All eyes turned upon him. He shifted his great bulk from one foot to the other. "Your majesty has a most adequate library," he continued. "We may not have it long, but it is still here. And there is a youth engaged in the business of cataloguing it so that the university at Heliopolis can make an offer for it. This youth comes from Jessamy—the son of an instrument-maker—and he has been attending the university on a grant which the government gave to him. It seems, you see, that this boy is of exceptional intelligence and aptitude. With the whole library at his disposal. . . ."

"Are you suggesting," said Rufus Malagig IV, "that Damian should *cheat?*"

"Not at all," said Coronado, stepping in hurriedly. "It is hardly cheating if the prince makes use of the . . . er . . . research facilities at his disposal. I think that the boy might well be regarded, for the time being, as . . . an extension of the library services. He will, after all, only be *assisting* the prince."

The king thought about it for a few moments, then nodded. He was realistic enough to know that there was no other way that the prince was going to answer any but the easiest questions.

"Suppose the enchanter finds out?" asked Damian, desperately.

"I think we can arrange that he won't," said the prime minister, smoothly. "We can, I think, conduct the whole affair by mail. If we write immediately to Sirion Hilversun requesting that he send us the first question by return of post, and promise to deliver the answer forty-eight hours later, together with *our* first question . . . and so on. I think we'll have all the time we need, and we can get the answers how we please."

"He is an enchanter, you know," said the king. "He may have ways of finding these things out."

"As a matter of fact," said Coronado, "I don't think that it will matter if he does. As I said, this is an old custom—probably no more than a formality. I don't suppose he minds *how* we get the answers."

"*I* mind," say Damian, hopefully. "I think it's dishonest."

"Shut up!" said the king. "You'll do as you're told."

Damian sighed heavily. It was certainly no bed of

roses being crown prince of Caramorn. Sometimes he wondered if he wouldn't have been better off cataloguing libraries or some other such thing.

Ewan was sitting quietly on a high stool between two colossal bookcases, reading by the light of a candle. It was the middle of the day, but the library windows were obscured by the ends of bookshelves, books stacked on the ledges, and by the dust of decades. The candle was necessary.

He was so engrossed that he did not hear the door open and close. He was reading an ancient text by a failed alchemist who attempted to show that lead was much more useful and of greater value than gold. Not until a shadow fell across the page, when Coronado moved between the candle-flame and the book, did he realize that he was no longer alone.

"Don't stand up," said the prime minister, in his best approximation of a friendly paternal tone.

"I'm sorry, sir," said Ewan. "I didn't hear you come in."

"Hard at work, eh?"

"Yes, sir." Ewan blushed suddenly. "I wasn't really reading it. Just—scanning through it. To see if . . ."

"Of course," purred the prime minister. "I understand perfectly. You have to describe books in your catalogue. The university want to know what they're buying. Don't worry a bit. You don't tell me how to be prime minister, I won't tell you how to catalogue a library, all right?"

Ewan grinned weakly. He had never talked to a prime minister before. He was not intimidated, but he did feel that Coronado's sickly tone of voice was unwarranted. Ewan didn't like people to speak to him as if he was a child.

"And how are you getting on?" asked Coronado.

"Very well, thank you, sir," replied Ewan.

"You'll get us a good price for it all, I hope."

"That's nothing to do with me," Ewan was quick to assure him. "I only list the books. The archivists at the university will check through it and decide what price to offer."

"Oh, to be sure, to be sure," murmured the prime minister, idly, maintaining the silky tone in his voice. His eyes ran over the shelves, noting the tide marks in the dust where books had been disturbed for the first time in more than a hundred years. The king and his forefathers had been great collectors, when they could afford the luxury, but very few people at the palace ever read anything except the newspapers. His gaze came to rest on the ink-pot and quill, which stood upon the parchment on which Ewan was compiling his list. To judge by the number of completed pages there was a very great deal of work still to be done.

Ewan blinked, wondering what so august a person could possibly want with him, not liking to ask.

"What do you do with your spare time?" asked the prime minister.

"I don't have a great deal," said Ewan.

"You enjoy your work?"

Ewan shrugged. "I like books. I like reading. I even like making lists. I don't mind working a long day. After all, it's for the good of the country, isn't it?" He supplemented this last remark with a weak smile, as though it were a joke—or perhaps half a joke.

"It is indeed," said Coronado soberly. "And that's something you care about, is it? The good of your country?"

"Of course," said Ewan. What else can you say to a prime minister who also happens to be your employer? But in point of fact, Ewan was being honest. Though he felt that his own future might lie in lands far to the west, he was concerned about Caramorn. His father and mother were here, and his two sisters, and everyone he had known as a boy. He knew about the bad harvests, and even felt slightly guilty that he had missed the worst of them by being away in the Western Empire, where food was plentiful.

"I'm glad," said Coronado. "Because it happens that there's a small favour you can do for your country. A little extracurricular task, as you might say. I can't offer you money, or any other material incentive, but I can assure you that if you do this little thing you'll have brought the country one step nearer to salvation from ruin. Will you do it?"

Ewan wanted to reply, as any sensible person would have: "That depends what it is." But it was such a nice speech, such a heartfelt appeal, that it would have seemed churlish and unpatriotic to prevaricate. So Ewan said, "I'll be glad to," just as Coronado had known that he would.

"That's excellent," said Coronado. "I'm afraid you'll be an unsung hero, because this must be kept very quiet. It's a state secret, in fact. You'll have nothing but the satisfaction of having helped your country, but for a man like yourself I know that will be enough. Now, I want you to swear that you'll never breathe a word of this to anyone. No one must ever know of your involvement."

Ewan felt a sinking feeling in his stomach. He knew that he was being used. The slickness of the prime minister's whole approach told him that something underhanded was going on. But he also knew that he had no choice. He had to play the game, whatever it was.

"Do you swear?" said Coronado.

"I swear," said Ewan, with the faintest of sighs.

"Well, then," continued the prime minister, leaning

over so that his lantern jaw was only a few inches from Ewan's ear, "it's like this. Prince Damian is in a bit of a spot. It is vitally necessary, for reasons of state, that he should marry a certain young lady. It was, for various reasons, necessary that we should arrange all this in a bit of a hurry. Naturally, both the young people concerned are a little apprehensive. They're a fraction reluctant. They don't really understand why things must move so fast, and apparently without much regard for their own feelings. You, of course, are an intelligent person and can see the logic of such arrangements, can understand the fact that sometimes a marriage must be made in order to help a kingdom out of its little difficulties.

"To cut a long story short, the other party—the young lady, that is—is prevaricating slightly. She says that she will marry the prince if he can answer three questions she will put to him, and has offered him the right to put three questions to her. This way, both young people have a chance to . . . er . . . make *sure* of one another. Win one another's respect, if you see what I mean. It's an old custom—perhaps you've read about it?"

"I believe I did," said Ewan, "somewhere . . ."

"Well," said Coronado. "Never mind trying to remember. The important thing is this. We need someone to give the prince a little *assistance*—answering the questions that are put to him and framing the ones which he shall put in his turn. *That* is where you come in."

"Ah," said Ewan, pensively.

"What do you think?" asked Coronado.

"Isn't it just a bit . . . a very little bit . . . dishonest?"

The prime minister drew himself up to his full height, and waved a large, bony hand imperiously. "Not at all," he said. "Not at all. We're merely taking advice. Taking advice is an accepted part of court protocol, recognized by every law and moral principle we have."

"Oh," said Ewan. He was dubious, but he knew that he was hardly in a position to argue. "What are the questions, then?"

"We don't know as yet. We're expecting the first one to arrive by express mail, first thing in the morning. We've agreed to take them one at a time, you see."

"I see," echoed Ewan, who didn't like the look of this at all.

"Look upon it as a challenge," suggested Coronado.

Ewan nodded.

"And always remember that it's for the greater good of Caramorn."

Ewan nodded again.

"And there is one more thing," added Coronado, as he began to move away, toward the door.

Ewan looked at him patiently, feeling that it was unnecessary to reply.

"You might care to bear in mind that in the present desperate state of emergency all government funds are frozen. Unless something happens to give Caramorn a considerable boost, it will not be possible for the state to renew any grants and suchlike during the coming year. If this marriage does not take place, I'm afraid there's a strong possibility that you might not be able to return to Heliopolis to continue your studies. So you *do* see how important this is, don't you?"

"Oh, yes," said Ewan, in a low voice. "I do see."

"I think we understand one another," said Coronado, making his exit smoothly and quietly.

"We certainly do," murmured Ewan, to the empty air. "We certainly do."

"MIRROR, MIRROR ON the wall," recited Helen, "what's the most difficult question of all?"

"I don't have to answer that," retorted the mirror. "And if I did I'd probably point out that the one you just asked me must be a candidate. What's more, it doesn't scan properly."

"Look," said Helen, with exasperation. "All I ask is a little co-operation. A little assistance. Advice, maybe. For old times' sake."

"Ha!" said the mirror.

"All I want," said Helen, controlling her voice to restore some of the natural sweetness to it, "is a few suggestions relating to unanswerable questions. It has to look reasonable, of course—the kind of question that seems simple enough but when you get right down to it is quite impossible."

"It's not my field," said the mirror. "I'm only here

to report on reflections. What you need is a paradox monger."

"What's a paradox monger?"

"Someone who sells paradoxes."

"And where, pray, am I going to find one of those?"

"Search me," said the mirror. "And stop doing that."

"What?"

"Trying to turn me off."

"Turn you off?" repeated Helen.

"You heard me," said the mirror.

"I'm not trying to turn you off."

"Yes, you are."

"No, I'm not."

There was a brief pause. Then the mirror said: "Well, somebody is. Look at yourself. Can't you see the image distorting?"

Helen looked at her face reflected in the glass. Now the mirror came to mention it there *was* something odd about it. It seemed blurred. She put her hand to touch the surface of the mirror, and the image put out *her* hand. But the other hand was somehow paler and less distinct. When her fingers touched the glass Helen could feel a faint but rather strange *electric* sensation.

"You're not breaking down, are you?" said Helen. "You're the last half-way reasonable magic mirror we've got."

"I'm in the best of health," said the mirror. "Someone's interfering with me, I tell you. I'm being got at. I feel distinctly dizzy, as if my reflection was whirling round and round.

This was perhaps not so surprising, because even as the mirror spoke the image reflected in it *did* begin to spin around and around. The blurs became streaks and the whole thing dissolved into a whirlpool of colour.

"Oooooh!" moaned the mirror. "Stop it. Please!"

"It isn't me," said Helen helplessly. "Honestly."

She wondered whether it might be her father. But Sirion Hilversun was not the kind of man to start working wayward magic in his daughter's bedchamber.

Suddenly, Helen felt frightened. She leapt to her feet and would have run to the door to call to her father, except that the whirling image began to slow down again and become distinct.

For a moment, she thought that the mirror was recovering, having suffered a dizzy spell or a mild fit of some kind, but then she realized that the face coalescing out of the blur was not her own. Most definitely not, in fact.

It was the face of an old man. A *very* old man. Sirion Hilversun was getting on two hundred by now, but compared to this face his was young. Sirion Hilversun's hair was white and his beard was long, but the hair retained a certain fluffiness, and his complexion was pleasantly pink. The man whose image was in the mirror now had hair the colour of ancient dust, a beard that seemed as insubstantial as morning mist. His skin was dark brown and looked to have the texture of varnished wood. The eyes were large and staring, and coloured a deep, deep purple. They had no whites at all, and the black pupils were very tiny. The expression worn by the face was neither hostile nor ugly, but it was nevertheless a very frightening face.

"Sit down," it said. Its voice was not the voice of the mirror, but deeper and somehow more remote.

"Who are you?" she whispered.

"It doesn't matter," he replied.

"What do you want?"

"I came in answer to your plea." There was the ghost of a smile in the thin, dark lips.

"What plea?"

"Questions," he said, simply. "You asked for questions. I bring you six. Six of the most curious questions in the world. No one has answered them in a hundred years and more. No one has dared to try."

"I don't need six," said Helen, uneasily. "Three at the most. If they're really unanswerable, one will do."

"You have to take the six," said the image, gently. "They come as a package, so to speak."

The image reached into the folds of its black cloak, and produced a scroll of yellow parchment. "I fear that I cannot pass this through the mirror," said the sonorous voice. "You will appreciate that I am only here, as it were, in spirit. I will hold it up. You must read it carefully—all of it. Its words will be impressed upon your memory. You will not forget."

"Wait . . ." said Helen, uneasily.

But the image wouldn't wait. Two skeletal brown hands unwound the parchment and held its face towards Helen. The vast purple eyes peered over the upper edge, focusing on Helen's face.

Helen read the words.

The parchment read:

THE LAST WILL AND TESTAMENT OF
JEAHAWN KAMBALBA

I leave to the world my fortune and my fate, these verses:

> What words are writ upon the stone
>   beneath the sign which stands alone
>   in Methwold forest held in thrall?
> And what are those engraved by me
>   on Faulhorn's horn which waits for thee
>   in Mirasol's haunted banquet hall?

Where the towers of Ora Lamae stood
a lamia waits to drink your blood—
what secret name is in her bred?
The monster Zemmoul takes his prey
where Fiora falls in silver spray—
what coloured gem is in his head?

If you take your stand in Hamur's place
at edge of world and gate of space—
what feeling creeps within your bone?
Aloof from Sheal the shadowed deep
at edge of world and gate of sleep—
what do you feel as you stand alone?

While Helen scanned these words, the stare of the
purple eyes never wavered. Only when she finished did
the intensity of the gaze relent somewhat.

Helen had held her breath for some time. Now she
let it out in a short, fearful gasp.

"That's a spell!" she said.

"It is indeed," said the image. "A very powerful spell."

"And you've printed it in my mind! You've made it
a part of me."

"Or you a part of it," answered the man with purple
eyes.

"I'll tell my father!"

The image shook its head. "No, my dear. You will
tell no one. This is a secret spell. Our secret."

"You can't *do* this...."

"I can. You prepared my ground. Perhaps I put the
idea into your head, but you spoke the words.... It was
you who sought to *use* the plan. Three questions are
yours, and three belong to another. That is the game.
You asked to play, and now you must."

"Who are you?" she demanded again. Then she remembered the name at the top of the parchment. Even while he was rolling it up again her eyes picked it out. "Jeahawn Kambalba!" she whispered. "Jeahawn the Judge! But he's been dead for . . ." she trailed off.

"As I said," the image reminded her, "I can be with you only in spirit. I am dead, but a little of me lives on — in the spells I cast and the implements I once owned. You knew, of course, that this mirror was once mine?"

Helen shook her head. "Father bought it at an auction," she said. "He was always buying things at auctions. After the war, you know. . . ."

Again, she stopped. Of course he knew. Wasn't it Jeahawn Kambalba that had put an end to the wars? Hadn't he imprisoned Elfspin and Ambrael, defeated Jargold?

"What do you want with me?" she whispered.

"Your help," he answered.

"I've no magic."

"Nor has the boy. And perhaps you have a little more than you know. The verses will tell you what you must do. I know you're frightened, but that will pass. I can't promise you definitely that no harm will come to you, because it might. I know that this is terribly unfair, but it has to be done. The one thing you need to know is that now the pattern is begun it *must* be completed. You understand that. You know the ways of enchantment. Look at me."

Unwillingly, she stared straight into the terrible eyes, which grew once again in intensity until they seemed almost luminous.

Helen's hand took up a pen from the table beside the bed, and a page of parchment, and she began to write. As soon as the letter was complete, the image began to fade, but Helen was still entranced. She put it in an envelope and sealed it in, and set it down in front of her. By this time the mirror was absolutely blank.

Then there was a small sound, like a polite cough. Helen woke, and in the mirror before her she saw her own image, clear and beautiful. She stared at it hard, trying to remember something—a dream or a reverie. She couldn't recall it, although she knew that it was still there, in her memory, waiting to be unlocked by the right key.

There was a knock on the door, and Sirion Hilversun came in.

"I really must have that letter now," he said. "They asked for a reply by return of post, and it's nearly bedtime."

Without a word, Helen handed him the envelope.

"You've sealed it!" exclaimed the enchanter. "Don't you want me to read it?"

"I'm sorry," she said, softly. "I must have done it absent-mindedly. But it doesn't matter. It's only a silly question. Quite trivial, really."

Sirion Hilversun frowned. He had harboured dark suspicions about what kind of questions his daughter might ask of Prince Damian. Now, it seemed, he wasn't to know.

"You are giving him a chance, aren't you?" he asked.

Helen turned to him, and smiled. She took his old, gnarled hand into her own, and squeezed it reassuringly. "Oh, yes," she said. "Every chance. All that it needs is a little initiative and..."

She stopped, frowning slightly as if trying to remember something that was scurrying away into the corridors of her mind.

"What, dear?" he prompted. "What were you going to say?"

"Judgement," she finished. "I was going to say ... judgement."

At noon the next day Coronado went to see Ewan, who was delving deep in the dustiest corners of the palace library, inspecting the titles and indices of books by the score and then stacking them neatly out of the way. His search was hurried, but marked by a systematic efficiency.

"Well?" inquired the prime minister.

"I'm tracking it down," said Ewan, without even turning his head. "Just give me time. I'm on the track."

Coronado nodded and left him to it.

At six in the evening the scene was repeated, just about word for word. The only difference was that by now Ewan was considerably dustier and the prime minister was a little worried.

At eleven, before the royal family retired for the night, Coronado tried again, hoping to discover some pleasant news for the king and the prince to sleep on. By this time Ewan was positively filthy, and every book in the library seemed to have been shifted and sorted.

"Don't worry," said the boy. "I've found a hundred books with references to Methwold forest. I'm going through the lot, word by word, if necessary. If the words on that stone were ever seen by human eyes I'll know what they were by morning."

The prime minister noted, however, that there was a definite note of optimistic strain in Ewan's voice. Though he said nothing he did not go to his bed filled with confidence. In point of fact, the only person in the palace who slept soundly was the queen, who secretly didn't want Damian to marry the girl at all. Damian himself slept badly because he still feared that Ewan *might* find the answer.

At nine the next morning, after breakfast, Coronado went back to the library, determined that this time there must be an answer ... or else. Or else what he hadn't quite decided.

Ewan was black from head to toe and looked very sleepy. He was also more than a little annoyed.

"It's not here," he said. "It's just not here. I've been through it all for nothing."

"Nothing?" repeated the prime minister, ominously.

Ewan looked up, and perceived that the other was not in the best of moods.

"*Almost* nothing," he said.

"What do you mean *almost?*" purred Coronado.

"Well," said Ewan. "I don't have the answer. But I have found something extremely curious." He took up an extremely ancient piece of parchment and passed it to Coronado.

The prime minister blew away a little spare dust and tried to read the words inscribed on the paper. He failed. The scribble *looked* like words, but there was something wrong with it.

"What is it?" he asked.

"Actually," said Ewan, "it's the question. Or, rather, a set of six questions, of which the one sent to us is the first."

"Are you telling me," said Coronado, his temper rising slightly, "that you've been in here twenty-four hours and all you have to show for it is another copy of the question?"

"Well," said Ewan, "if you want to put it like that, I suppose the answer is *yes*. But it's a very curious piece of paper, I think you'll agree."

"I can't even read it," said Coronado.

"That's because it's been turned round," said Ewan. "It's written backwards—as though it were a mirror-image of itself, if you see what I mean."

Coronado did see what he meant. But he didn't see what help it was.

"Does this help us to solve the problem?" he asked, trying to keep his voice very level.

"Not exactly," said Ewan. "But it is interesting. You see, these verses are the words of one Jeahawn Kambalba, who was a famous enchanter of long ago. This is his so-called last will and testament—it's a notorious enigma. No answer has ever been recorded because no one ever dared to tamper with the work of such a powerful man. Superstition, you see, kept people clear of it."

"What you're trying to say . . ." began Coronado.

". . . is that no one knows the answer," Ewan finished for him. "It seems to me that the young lady has deliberately sent Prince Damian a question which she believes to be unanswerable."

Coronado felt a terrible sense of impending disaster. This was exactly what he had feared. He gritted his teeth.

"In that case," he said, "we shall have to adopt what we in political circles call a *contingency plan.*"

"You mean," said Ewan, "that you're going to make up an answer and send it back hoping that she doesn't know the right answer any more than we do?"

Coronado's eyebrows slowly elevated themselves to the region of his hairline.

"They did say you were a very clever boy," he murmured.

"It's not necessary," said Ewan.

The eyebrows descended like falling logs. "What do you mean?"

"I mean that we aren't finished yet. Methwold forest is only half a day's ride from here. I can be there and back by nightfall. All I have to do, I reckon, is go there, find the signpost, and look at the stone."

Coronado moved his lantern jaw slowly from side to side, ruminatively. After a brief pause, he said: "You know what you're suggesting?"

"Of course," answered Ewan.

"Methwold forest is over the border. In the magic lands. It's enchanted. No one ever goes there. It's said that the last half a dozen men who even went near it failed to return. There's no daylight inside the forest, and it's full of trolls and tree spirits. Not to mention poisonous snakes. It's not the place to go for a picnic." Coronado paused, wondering whether he ought to stop trying to talk the boy out of it. Then he went on: "The thing is, boy . . . I rather like you. You have the makings of a politician. You're no fool. You know which side your bread's buttered. Take a tip from me—in a situation like this you always try the tricks of the trade first. Let's try the contingency plan, eh?"

"It might not work," said Ewan. "Sirion Hilversun is an enchanter. He may know what's on the stone even if no ordinary eye has ever seen it. He may have . . . ways . . . of finding out."

Coronado nodded, slowly. "It's a risk," he admitted. "But so is going into the enchanted forest. I'm a politician. I only take political risks. Only a hero or a fool would take the other one." While he spoke his eyes lingered on Ewan's dust-stained face. Is this a hero? wondered the prime minister. Or a fool?

"I want to go," said Ewan.

Coronado thought quickly. Discretion might be best. If the king found out, he might think that Coronado himself had asked or ordered the boy to risk his neck. The king had quite a sentimental streak when it came to the welfare of his subjects. This was better kept quiet.

"Well," he said, eventually, "they collected the horses yesterday, I'm afraid. There's only a couple left. Two carthorses and an old grey mare who hasn't enough years left in her to make it worth transporting her all the way to Heliopolis. I suppose you'd better take her. But go quickly and quietly. And remember . . . it's your own idea. I advised you against it."

"That's all right," said Ewan. "After all, it's for the good of the kingdom, isn't it?"

"Definitely," confirmed Coronado.

"And just between you and me," said the boy, "we both know who'd take the blame if we submitted a fake answer and it all went wrong. Don't we?"

The prime minister's eyebrows quivered restlessly. "We *do* understand one another," he said, softly. "Don't we?"

Ewan beat a little of the dust from his jerkin. It didn't seem to make much difference. He moved past the prime minister and headed for the door.

"I'll see you tonight," he said. "With the answer."

"I believe you will," murmured Coronado. "I do believe you will."

{6}

IT TOOK LONGER than Ewan expected to get to Methwold forest. The aged grey mare which he had borrowed set off at a good enough stride but tired very quickly. She was doing her best, but her best was a very laboured trot, and even that could be maintained only for a few minutes at a time. He had hoped to arrive at his destination by noon, but the afternoon was well under way by the time he did get there.

He soon found out, however, that the time of day was irrelevant inside the forest itself. Most of what Coronado had said Ewan had dismissed as superstition and rumour, but one thing, at least, was true. Once within the shadow of the trees the light faded dramatically.

Even though he had given Coronado's dire warning little credence, Ewan had had the good sense to take one elementary precaution. He had brought a lantern, consisting of a candle mounted in a glass casket with a hole on top to let the smoke out. As soon as it became obvious that the great canopy made by the foliage of the trees would let little or no light reach the forest floor, Ewan lit the candle.

The wan yellow light seemed to make the shadows that gathered around so much more dense and menacing, but another half-furlong would leave the last tiny rays of sunshine long behind, and candlelight was infinitely preferable to Stygian gloom. Ewan leaned forward to stroke the mare's neck reassuringly, and the mare turned to look at him over her shoulder. She looked apprehensive.

"It's okay," he assured her. "If there *are* any trolls and the like, which I doubt, it'll have been so long since they saw a boy or a horse that we'll probably scare them half to death."

The mare grunted non-committally.

The road across the magic land had so far been a good one—better than the dirt track that ran this way from Jessamy. It had once been firm and polished, but the times of strife had seen it cracked and worn, and it was hardly as good as new. Nevertheless, it was easy to follow and offered secure footing for a horse. In the forest, though, the road ended, and there was nothing at all beyond it to mark a way: not even an animal track.

"It isn't going to be easy to find a signpost where there aren't any roads," observed Ewan, chewing his lower lip. The mare made no comment.

The world inside Methwold forest was not as he had imagined it might be. In his mind the word "forest" was associated with greenery and birdsong, the rustle of small creatures in the grass, and tall, round-boled trees. He had expected an enchanted forest to be a little less pleasant, but not so totally different. Inside Methwold, the basic colour was grey. The trees were gnarled and twisted, their trunks and branches made up of thin elements coiled and bundled together. No birds sang, and where there was the noise of movement near the ground it was always the sound of *slithering*.

The trees were living, as was proved by the uncannily rich foliage which they produced, but seen from beneath they seemed as if they were being slowly consumed by decay. Their bark looked soft, and was overlaid by some greasy substance. As well as a multitude of little wrinkled leaves the branches were festooned by silvery networks like garments spun by giant spiders.

All in all, it was quite unearthly.

On either side of Ewan's path, as he picked his way between the trees, was a tangled network of plants which grew, at first, only as high as the horse's withers, but which seemed higher and denser the further they progressed. It looked very soft, and was certainly not impenetrable, but as time went by Ewan got the distinct feeling that it was forming *walls* on either side of him, guiding him. He contemplated turning aside to force the mare through it, but hesitated because of an uncomfortable suggestion somewhere at the back of his mind that it would suck him in like quicksand, cling to him and hold him fast. It looked like a mixture of cobweb and candlewax, and he was afraid of it because he did not know what kind of plant could grow in perfect darkness.

He looked carefully around and saw that this gentle barrier did, indeed, form a kind of corridor into which he had been unwittingly guiding the mare. Because he could not overcome his reluctance to defy its guidance and crash into or through it, there seemed to be little option but to follow it further. So he did. And as he did, the wall grew still higher and thicker, until it was at the level of his shoulder—and yet further, until it merged with low branches and the silvered foliage.

He had no idea whether the course he was keeping was straight or not, and he harboured dire suspicions as to where the corridor might be leading him.

He patted the patient mare yet again, though it was he that needed the reassurance. "If we ever come back here," he murmured, "I want you to remind me of the old saying. A fool rushes in, but an angel carries a compass. Will you do that?"

The mare made no answer.

Ewan held the lantern a little lower to pick out the ground on which the grey mare trod. Scattered in his path was a carpet of toadstools, with caps that were grey and peeling, or blue and lustrous, or sometimes dark red and warty. All manner of similar fungi grew in the crevices of the gnarled trunks and at the junctures where branch-elements spiralled off into the tangled skeins. They were often coloured, but never brightly—instead they were faded and dull and darkened and dim.

Ewan had never felt quite so lonely.

"You see," he began to explain to the mare, "why people think this place is haunted. It does give that impression, although it's all really perfectly natural. One can understand how these susperstitions start. At least, I can. I suppose that being a horse you don't worry too much over these intellectual niceties, do you?"

The old grey mare sniffed and grated her teeth a little.

"I couldn't agree more," muttered the boy. "If an owl hooted right now I'd jump out of my skin."

He paused, as if expecting an owl to hoot on cue, but no owl did. He listened carefully, but all he could hear was the sound of *slithering*.

He gulped.

"If I were of a nervous disposition," said Ewan, "I'd begin to worry right now about that old tale people tell about the way that roads in enchanted forests just go round and round, so that once in you can never get out. I suppose this *is* a road, of a sort . . . or a tunnel . . . or something."

While he spoke, the grey mare plodded on.

And the soft walls seemed, now that they had stopped growing upwards, to be drawing ever closer.

"It's a curious illusion," commented Ewan, "that parallel lines seem to meet at infinity. If you stand in the middle of a straight road, it seems to get ever narrower as it extends to the horizon. I've often wondered why."

The mare ducked her head and shook it slightly.

"You always wondered why as well, eh?" said Ewan.

In all probability, the old mare had meant nothing of the kind. But either way, the fact remained that the route *was* getting narrower, and it wasn't an illusion.

Somewhere off to the right, and then, again, to the left, there was a slow, stretching sound of sinuous *slithering*.

"I don't know about you," muttered Ewan, patting the mare's neck furiously, "but I'm terrified."

The way became so constricted that the tangled branches formed a matted roof just above Ewan's head. The longest and limpest reached out to trail clammy tips along his arms and shoulders, and *tap, tap, tap* at the glass casket holding the valiant candle. This was a tunnel indeed—a horrid, soft-walled tunnel. And he came, eventually, to a place where there was no longer room for a boy on horseback to proceed.

There were only two options open to him. He could try to go back. Or he could go on foot.

He backed up three paces until there was room for

him to dismount in the confined space between the mare's flank and the glutinous wall. He went on alone, and the pale yellow light of the candle seemed to him to be the most precious thing in the world. In point of fact, as he walked alone in the enchanted forest, there *was* only one other thing that he could call his own, and that was a set of panpipes he carried in his pocket—a small present from his father, the maker of musical instruments.

He looked back once, but the mare was already out of sight. He listened for the sound of her whinnying, or even the sound of her grinding her teeth . . . but there was nothing. Except, of course. . . .

But he shut his ears to *that* sound and went on.

And on.

And on.

The little toadstools broke beneath his feet and were squashed into pulp.

Ewan kept licking his lips. He wanted to talk, to let some of the tension that was tightening his every muscle ebb away in the sound of his voice, but the grey mare was no longer there, and for some unknown reason he could not bring himself to talk to the empty air. It was not that he was afraid that no one was listening . . . but rather the reverse. . . .

The silence was unbearable, and that *other* sound, when it came, even more so. The only course possible was to take out the little reed pipes and begin to play.

Considering that he was the son of an instrument-maker and had grown up surrounded by devices for making music, Ewan was not very good. There were a number of simple tunes he could pick out on any of a dozen instruments, but they were repetitive dance tunes and the rhythms of nursery rhymes. He knew nothing that really seemed appropriate to his present predicament. He could manage no stirring martial music, nor anything soft and beautiful.

And so he played "Baa, baa, black sheep" instead.

In situations like his, you have to do what you can.

He played it over and over and over. There was no one to sing the words, but he imagined them inside his head. He also imagined children dancing to the sound. At first it was just his little sisters, but then he added himself and his mother and his father. After a while, he brought in a few passers-by, and then invented a carnival troupe. He realized that the process could go on for ever, and ultimately he had the entire population of Jessamy, including the ministers and the royal family, dancing in his head to "Baa, baa black sheep." As an afterthought, for good measure, he added a trio of trained elephants and the old grey mare.

He didn't count the paces he took or keep any track of time. He just kept on, and he ignored the fact that he was dog tired and that his feet ached terribly. He might have gone on for ever.

Eventually, though, he had to pause. His fingers and his lips just couldn't keep it up. "Baa, baa black sheep" stopped. The dancing horde inside his head stopped, and then faded away. Into the silence there came a new noise— neither the neigh of a horse nor the perpetual *slithering*.

It was laughter.

Cool, cruel, cackling laughter.

And it came from behind him.

A bolt of fear struck straight into his heart. He could feel the blood pounding in his veins. He couldn't bear to look back. He knew he had to, but he couldn't.

The *slithering* was suddenly loud and all around him, mingling with the laughter, mixing and dissolving into it. He realized at last what the *slithering* was.

It was the branches, creeping like snakes, writhing as they knotted and kneaded, tangled and touched, quivered and quaked.

And the laughter was the laughter of a million shivering leaves, rattling and chuckling, rustling and giggling.

Then a branch reached out, closed cobwebbed finger-leaves about the wick of the candle, reaching through the hole cut in the glass.

The light went out.

Ewan quivered, just once. He felt faint. He dropped the lantern. He stood quite still and waited.

Soon, he realized that he could see again, by pale greenish-white light. The branches of the terrible trees were alive, not merely with their own sinuous movement, but with glow-worms that crawled from every crack and cranny. They came from the murky depths which surrounded him to make a cocoon of radiance.

He looked round, awed and quite unable to understand.

The way ahead was still waiting. But it was no longer a tunnel getting ever narrower and leading nowhere. It was a doorway to a clearing. In the clearing, illumined by a chandelier of glow-worm infested branches, was a mound of stones, and supported by the mound of stones was a signpost.

It was the weirdest signpost that Ewan had ever seen. Its arms hung limp and were crumpled, as if half melted by great heat at some time in the indeterminate past. Its stem was bent over, so that two of its arms pointed down, two up.

Ewan walked into the clearing, and the gateway behind him sealed itself silently. But he was past fear by now. He was quite calm.

He walked forward and began to rummage among the rounded stones which formed the cairn beneath the signpost. It didn't take more than a minute to find the stone that he wanted. It was in no way similar to the rest. It was flat and square and pale blue in colour. It was polished smooth, and engraved upon it were the following words:

TURN THE SIGNPOST ROUND

And that, thought Ewan, dazedly, is *that*. So much for one of the great mysteries of our time.

But it was not so simple.

He had, by some peculiar quirk of fate, been allowed to reach his destination just as it seemed the forest would not let him . . . but getting there was only half the battle.

The question now was: how did he propose to get back?

He looked around and saw that the clearing was ringed by a solid wall of tangled branches, utterly impenetrable. He looked up and found that he could see dim and distant stars in the circle of night sky which the clearing cut out of the forest canopy. But that was no use. He couldn't fly.

Nowhere in the confining walls was there the slightest chink. There was not the thinnest sliver of empty shadow. There was no way out of the grim and gloomy prison.

Unless. . . .

He leapt suddenly up on to the mound of stones and grasped the bent stem of the signpost in both hands.

It turned quite easily. He turned it round one quarter of the way, and nothing changed. Then he turned it halfway round, and then three-quarters. Still nothing happened, and so he completed the operation, bringing the stem back to its original position.

Then it came alive in his hands.

There was a blinding flash as if lightning had struck into the clearing. Ewan's body jerked rigid with the shock. It was as though there was an explosion inside his head.

He toppled slowly from the mound to fall unconscious on to lush green grass.

Much later, he awoke.

It was late evening. The sun was sinking toward the western horizon. The sky was deep blue. Everything was bright.

Everything. . . .

The signpost stood tall and straight, its four arms pointing along four neatly cut tracks extending into the forest. The forest was green, its trees standing tall and dignified, no longer involved in a conspiracy to cut out every last vestige of the sunlight. Around the signpost grasses grew, and there were flowers on the forest floor. The sound of birdsong was dancing in the air.

Leaves rippled, and the undergrowth rustled with the passage of small creatures. As Ewan sat up and looked round, a butterfly which had settled on his sleeve took off and bobbed in the air as it steered itself to a nearby cluster of willow-herb. There was a sweet smell on the drifting wind. A small stream emerged from the other side of the moss-covered cairn to run away downhill towards the edge of the world.

Ewan wondered desperately what day it was. If it was the same day that he had set out, he could be in time with the answer when he returned to Jessamy. If it was the day after, then he had run over the time limit. He remembered the patch of night sky that he had seen before turning the signpost around. It *had* to be the next day. He must have been asleep for many, many hours.

But something inside him told him that it *wasn't* the

next day, that he still had time.

He stood up and stretched his limbs.

The grey mare was standing beside one of the four roads which led away into the forest—the one which led away toward the setting sun, and Caramorn. In the grass where he had lain were two things. One was a set of panpipes. The other was a candle in a glass casket. When he knelt to pick them up he saw, much to his surprise, that the wick of the candle was still smouldering.

While he marvelled, he heard the sound of someone approaching. Coming from the east, walking beside the little stream, was a figure bent with age, cloaked and hooded, helping himself along with a long black staff which seemed to be carved out of ebony wood.

Ewan ran to the man's side, and without bothering with any formula of greeting, said: "Tell me quickly, please—what day is this?"

The bent figure unwound slightly, and the light penetrated the shadow within the hood just long enough for Ewan to catch the merest glimpse of two remarkable eyes.

"You are in time," said the hooded man. Just that, and no more.

Ewan did not pause but ran back to the mare and mounted her. He had turned her towards Jessamy and urged her into her shambling trot before it occurred to him that the answer he had received was really no answer at all. How could the old man possibly have known why he needed to know what day it was?

He looked back quickly, but the hooded figure was no longer to be seen. Ewan shook his head, wonderingly. He was angry at himself for having taken the answer at face value like that. He had simply accepted it, and trusted it, without a moment's thought.

And yet, inside himself, he still felt that it was true. He *would* be in time.

"Even so," he said, aloud, while he reached forward to pat the old grey mare on the neck, "remind me to ask my questions more carefully next time we meet a man with purple eyes."

WHILE HELEN STUDIED the letter her facial expression registered puzzlement and dismay.

It said, simply:

My dearest Helen,

The words written upon the stone beneath the signpost at the heart of Methwold forest were: TURN THE SIGNPOST ROUND. My question, obviously, is: "And what are those engraved . . . on Faulhorn's horn . . . in Mirasol's haunted banquet hall?" I trust you will find this query simple enough, as I found mine. I look forward to hearing your answer in two days' time.

Yours very sincerely, with all best wishes.

Damian, prince of Caramorn

"I just don't believe it," murmured Helen. "It's a lie. He made it up."

Tears came into her eyes, though she wasn't quite sure why. Partly it was annoyance, but partly it was the knowledge that she had somehow missed the target badly, and that she was now enmeshed by the consequences of her actions.

She saw her father hurrying across the great hall, and she quickly folded up the letter and put it away.

"The most *incredible* thing..." he began, and then broke off. "Was that the letter from Prince Damian?"

"Yes," she said, dully.

"May I see it?"

"Oh, no," she said, hurriedly. "It contains his question. You're bound to know the answer. I must find it myself."

"I won't tell you what it is."

"You know perfectly well that you wouldn't be able to resist the temptation to drop hints," she said, firmly. "I can't let you see it."

"Oh, well," sighed the enchanter. "But this does mean, doesn't it, that he answered your first question correctly?"

"Oh, yes," said Helen, dryly. "He answered it."

"I'm *so* glad. Everything is going very well, isn't it? You know, I was almost afraid that you'd attempt to set a question that was virtually unanswerable. I'm glad you're playing fair."

Helen looked down at the floor, as if inspecting the carpet for stains.

"You will be able to answer the prince's question, won't you?" asked Sirion Hilversun. "It's not too hard for you?"

She looked up at that, her eyes flaring as if she were

about to lose her temper. But she only said, in a voice steeped in determination: "His question is no harder than mine. If Prince Damian can discover what I set him to find, then there's no reason at all why I shouldn't succeed just as well."

"Oh, *good!*" said the enchanter. "Excellent!"

Helen managed a weak smile.

"What's incredible?" she asked.

"Eh?"

"You came in just now and said that something was incredible."

"Did I *really?*" The enchanter furrowed his brow stroked his long beard, thinking hard. He took a pair of spectacles out of his sleeve, polished them, and put them on. Then he peered all around the room. No inspiration struck him.

"I wonder what it was?" he murmured. "Quite slipped my mind. I wonder if it's something that's already happened or something's that's just about to happen. What do you think?"

"I don't know what to think," muttered Helen. "But don't worry about it. It'll be just as incredible when it occurs to you again, if not more so."

She made as if to leave, but Sirion Hilversun said: "No, wait. It'll come back. I was up on the battlements, pacing. I was looking out toward Methwold. Everything was just the same as usual. . . . I must have turned round half a dozen times. You know how it is when you're preoccupied . . . you see what you expect to see, not what's really there. But I finally noted that something wasn't as it should be, that something unfamiliar had turned familiar. . . ."

"The forest. . ." whispered Helen.

"That's right," said the enchanter, snapping his fingers. "The forest. It's turned green. Incredible! The enchanted forest has simply been ... *disenchanted!* I can't remember anything like it ever happening again. Or before, for that matter. Where are you going?"

"Out for a walk," said Helen, who was running towards the great staircase, intending to change her clothes immediately. "Maybe I'll go over the hill and out towards Mirasol."

"Oh, yes," said the enchanter, absently. "Good idea."

Meanwhile, in the library at the palace, while Ewan proceeded patiently with his task of cataloguing the books, Coronado was having his doubts.

"I admit that it was the obvious thing to do," he said. "But where would politics be if we never looked beyond the obvious? I think that we should have found an easier question. Nothing too fancy, just something ingenious and clever. We do, when all's said and done, want this marriage to take place."

"I answered the first question," pointed out Ewan. "It was pretty hairy there, for a while, but I did it. There's nothing impossible about the rhyme. And, as you agreed yourself when you wrote the letter out, the girl has laid down a challenge and we should be prepared to meet it. If we break the pattern she may decide that Damian is a worthless specimen and set something *really* hard next time."

"You have thought ahead, I suppose?" said Coronado sarcastically.

"About the lamia in the forbidden city? Certainly I have. And also about the gate at the edge of the world. I don't say I'm not worried. But when things got to their worst in that forest last night ... or tonight, perhaps, if I really did come back in time ... someone or something helped me. There's something very peculiar about that so-called will, and I can't help being curious."

"Curious enough to look up a lamia? Do you know what a lamia is?"

Ewan shrugged. "Supposedly a female vampire who may sometimes change into a snake."

"And that doesn't worry you?" asked the prime minister.

"I always suspect that such legends and rumours are wildly exaggerated," said Ewan. "As in the case of the forest, where men had disappeared and there were supposed to be trolls and evil spirits round every corner. It was just dark and rather nasty, that's all. And even that turned out to be an illusion that collapsed when I did something very simple."

"That may be very true," said Coronado. "And it's certainly brave. But if I were you, I wouldn't bank on that theory. It's never safe to mess about with the supernatural."

Ewan shrugged again. "The supernatural is only the natural we don't yet know much about," he said. "It's mostly to do with appearances, not with real things at all. Haven't you ever seen a conjurer at work?"

This remark had a slight hint of insult about it, but Coronado diplomatically let it go.

"I told the king where you'd been and what you'd done," mused Coronado. "He wasn't very happy about it. I didn't tell him about the rest of the verses. It didn't seem to be the right time. Deep down, you know, I'm not at all sure that he wants this to go through. I almost think that he'd like to find a legitimate excuse to call it off. The battle of conscious desires and unconscious prejudices, you know."

"I know," said Ewan. "Only too well. *My* conscious

desire tells me to get out of this now, and never mind the consequences. But there's something inside me that won't let it go. This is *important*. I think it's one of those things that once you're involved with it you can't back out. Do you see what I mean?"

"Certainly. It's like being prime minister of Caramorn. I have to save the kingdom, if only to protect my reputation. It's difficult to get another job if the last one ended in total disaster. I don't think I'm ready to retire yet, and the government couldn't pay my pension anyway."

"It's a hard life," commented Ewan, in a voice not overburdened with sympathy.

"It certainly is," said the elder statesman, shuffling away towards the door. As he went into the corridor he was desperately trying to think of another way—preferably an easier one. It was nice, he thought, to be a man with power—a man steering his own course through life towards a self-selected destiny. But it took a great deal of effort to steer, and the sea of life seemed full of the most wicked rocks and reefs.

This kingdom, he thought, doesn't deserve a man like me. And I certainly don't deserve a kingdom like this. Why, oh why, couldn't I have gone west years ago?

He realized that in his inmost thoughts he didn't really believe that a marriage between Damian and Helen would ever take place, or that it could save the kingdom if it did.

"No good will come of it all," he muttered beneath his breath. "No good at all. But when your back's to the wall, you have to try, haven't you?"

In the council chamber he found Alcover practising dealing cards from the bottom of a deck and Hallowbrand earnestly studying a cookery book in lieu of food.

"Where's Bellegrande?" he asked.

"Set out for Heliopolis this morning," grunted Al-cover. "Said he was going to try to negotiate some foreign aid. If you ask me he's trying to get a job as a translator or something."

Coronado groaned as things began to seem even blacker.

It looked as though the rats were about to start leaving the sinking ship.

UNLIKE MOONMANSION, WHICH was only a fake, Castle Mirasol had a moat, and also a great wooden drawbridge to span it. The moat had long ago dried up, but it still represented a barrier. The drawbridge was up and could only be let down from the inside.

Helen sat down at the edge of the moat and looked up at the ivied grey walls, whose worn battlements loomed high above her. The day was sullen and overcast, with rainclouds gathering ominously overhead. It was not the kind of day one would normally choose for a pleasant walk—or, for that matter, a heroic adventure—but Helen had not had the opportunity to pick and choose.

She wore a heavy jacket, denim jeans and pair of sensible shoes, so she wasn't unduly worried about the weather, but she was apprehensive lest her father should wonder why she had come out on such a day. He had ways of finding such things out. She was also worried about the problem of getting into Castle Mirasol. She wasn't afraid. She knew the castle was haunted, but she was too familiar with ghosts to let that worry her. Her anxiety was simply caused by the practical difficulties of getting in.

Had she been possessed of a more powerful species of magic there would have been any number of ways of gaining ingress. But she hadn't even sufficient power to motivate a broomstick—she had never wielded anything larger than an enchanted feather duster by the power of mind alone. She contemplated descending into the moat and attempting to climb the wall, but it was an awfully long way, and the slimed mud at the bottom of the moat smelled quite foul.

She sighed. "It will have to be cotton climbing, I suppose," she muttered.

So saying, she took from her jacket pocket a reel of black cotton, a darning needle, a wooden peg and a large hairpin. She put the peg through the hole in the reel and stuck it firmly into the ground. She unwound a few inches of cotton and bit it off, then tied the new end of the cotton still on the reel to the eye of the darning needle. She opened up the hairpin and forced the halves back against the bend, then made a tiny bow out of it by tying on the detached piece of cotton very tightly. She tested the strength of the bow, then placed the darning needle on it, as if it were an arrow.

She closed her eyes, and muttered: *"Bow bend, arrow fly, up and over, nice and high."* It was a very feeble spell, but it was one of the easiest in the book, and she had used it before.

The bow came alive in her hands, bent itself back, and then hurled the needle high into the air. The cotton reel spun on the slender peg as the cotton unravelled, and a black line whipped up into the sky. The needle disappeared over the battlements, and within a couple of seconds the reel was still. Helen drew the cotton taut and fastened it to the head of the peg, murmuring: *"Needle stick and stay secure, make my passage safe and sure."*

There was only one more conjuration needed, and she rattled it off: *"Cotton black and strong as steel, bear me up on an even keel."* Then she began climbing.

She was a good climber, but it was a long way, and a piece of cotton, strong as steel or not, is by no means as easy to grip as a thick rope. It didn't cut into her flesh as ordinary cotton would have cut into the flesh of someone without a modicum of magical protection, but it was difficult to manage. Had the spell not included a balancing clause she might never have made it.

Castle Mirasol looked forbidding from the outside, but when Helen peered down into the courtyard within, it seemed three or four times as bad. It was like looking down into a great black well. Although it was mid-afternoon the pale light of the glowering sky made little impression on the deep shadows which gathered inside the castle. They were shadows of incalculable age, which had enjoyed domination over the grey stone walls for a long, long time. It would take a strong light indeed to challenge them now. They were massive shadows, deep and solid, within which might lurk horrors unimaginable.

Everything was quite still . . . but not quite silent.

Far, far below—so far that it might emanate from the ultimate dungeons of the castle or the bowels of the Earth itself—there was a faint, uneasy sound of moaning.

The great hall, Helen knew, would be on the opposite side of the courtyard, its doors facing the drawbridge and the portcullis. But the only staircase descending from the ledge inside the battlements was on this side, zig-zagging down the corner of the north-west tower. She would have to go down, passing through the shadows which hung batlike from the walls, and then walk diagonally across the open space, immersed in the gloomy miasma, to the entrance of the hall. What she would find inside it she didn't know.

There was no point in hanging about. She walked to the head of the stair and began the descent.

There was no guard-rail on the stairway, and the steps were only two-and-a-half-feet wide. If she stumbled and chanced to fall over the edge she would plunge into the depths. She didn't intend to fall.

But the steps were covered in dust—a dust that was not fine and grey and powdery but thick and clotted and rather slimy. It was not nice to walk on, and, what was worse, it wasn't safe.

By the time she reached the tenth step, Helen was treading very carefully indeed, placing each leading foot so that the sole was using all the width of the step, in the middle of the span. As the murk gathered about her and the great dome of the sky became a crenellated square cut out by the battlements, she gradually became aware of things *moving* in the greasy grime—worms which wriggled beneath her heels, trying to get out of the way. The feeling was quite repulsive.

Every thirteen steps the stairway turned back on itself diagonally, so that she had to change direction. At every turn there was a flat ledge about six feet square. Where each of these ledges met the wall there were spider-webs three or four feet in diameter. Once or twice she saw the spiders lurking in crevices at the edges of the webs: vast black beings with bodies the size of fists and legs like great crippled fingers. The first time she caught sight of

one she gasped—not so much in fear as in loathing—
but not one of them moved. Even when, at the fifth
turning, the edge of her foot brushed and stirred an unusually large web, the builder of the web remained quite
still.

It occurred to her that the webs, like the stair itself,
were of incalculable age. In centuries none had caught
so much as a single fly. Even flies stayed clear of places
such as this. The spiders were all dead. They had died
at their stations.

Now, only their ghosts scuttled from shadow to
shadow, dark and silent. But Helen saw no spider-ghosts.
One never *does* see the ghosts of such creatures, which
have a preference for living *inside* walls and stones and
wooden things.

The square of grey sky slowly dwindled in size, and
its light—never powerful—retreated further and further
from the world which now surrounded Helen. When she
reached the bottom of the staircase it was very dark
indeed. She took from her pocket a box of matches
and struck one on the sandpaper side of the box. She
shut her eyes and muttered a swift spell: *"Match burn
bright and match burn long, guide me well and I won't
go wrong."* Then she set off across the open space.

There were no webs here, but the grease-laden dust
was still everywhere. The courtyard was paved with blocks
four feet by four, with the gaps filled in with cement,
but with time the cement had worn away, and grooves
in the slick black coat etched out the pattern perfectly.

She had gone no more than four or five paces when
the gleam of the match picked out something lying in
the dust. It was a lump, about the size of a human foot.
It may once have had shape and colour, but no longer.
It was amorphous, anonymous. Helen did not pause to

investigate. Another pace, and the matchlight found another, and yet another step took her within sight of three more. She picked her way carefully between them, careful not to step on one. In the centre of the courtyard there were so many that it was not easy to select a course.

In the very middle of the courtyard stood the castle well—a cylinder of brown brick with four upright wooden beams supporting a conical roof. The spindle was still there, and so was the rope wound around it, dangling into the well. Whether the bucket remained on the end of the rope was anyone's guess. On top of the well's roof was a model of a weathervane, with little bronze arrows pointing out the four different directions and a model of a little man blowing a great horn which would have swivelled to find the direction of the wind if ever a wind could blow down here in the belly of the castle.

Helen guessed readily enough that the model represented the giant Faulhorn, who had been killed long ago by the one-time owner of Castle Mirasol, King Belek of Beauval, who had become involved in the initial dispute between Elfspin and Viranian owing to the indiscretions of his own enchanters. Castle Mirasol had been the scene of one of the first great battles of the war, and had not been the same since.

Helen looked closely at the weathervane, in case this small replica of the giant's horn might also have words written upon it, but it didn't. She went on across the open space, still avoiding the shapeless things embedded in the dirt. At the mighty oaken doors of the great hall she paused again.

The distant moaning of the ghosts was not so distant now, and though it could still be heard emanating from far beneath her feet, it was now supplemented by a faint hollow whisper that came from within the hall.

It was not a loud sound but it was a complex one. It was not the work of one voice or even a hundred, but of a great multitude, most of whom were no doubt situated much more deeply than this, though a substantial fraction must be gathered in the great hall.

Helen gripped the handle of one of the big doors firmly in her left hand (the right held aloft the still-glimmering match) and turned it. Then she put her shoulder to the oaken panel and heaved with all her might.

Slowly and ponderously the door yielded and swung inwards.

She found that there were, indeed, five hundred or a thousand ghosts waiting for her within.

Ghosts are sometimes called shades or shadows, but that is exactly what they are *not*. Ghosts live in shadows, and stand out in their environment precisely because they themselves are composed of *unshadow*. Shadows are black and ghost gleam. A well-established ghost (recent ghosts are tentative and irregular in their manifestations) may be the purest glittering silver, shining very softly with a weird radiance quite unlike any other light which exists.

The ghosts which haunted the hall of Castle Mirasol were well established indeed. They were brilliant. Had this been any other kind of light it would have filled the hall with brightness and clarity, but it is the fate of ghosts always to be imprisoned by shadow and helpless within it . . . and hence the hall was a chaotic confusion of black and silver—deepest black and brightest silver, ghosts and shadows bound inextricably together.

The ghosts were seated about seven great tables—six set parallel to one another and in line with the door, and one at the far end, elevated somewhat and set at right angles. The tables had once been set with a glorious banquet, but that had been a very long time ago. The food had all rotted, unconsumed, and even the silver dishes and the forks and spoons were black with tarnish, while the copper candlesticks were green with verdigris except where their ruddiness was protected by translucent drips of wax from long-dead candles.

As Helen came into the hall every ghostly eye was turned upon her. Ghosts' eyes gleam more brightly than the rest of them, and sometimes seem like fiery diamonds when they are directed at a mortal being.

Helen paused, feeling the worms beneath her feet struggling to escape from their entrapment.

"Hello," she said. She was always polite to ghosts. It cost nothing.

There was no reply. The whispering had died away, though there was still the moaning from far below. Ghosts have the ability to stifle their otherwise perpetual voices when living creatures are about. It is probably a great relief to them.

"I won't disturb you," said Helen. "All I want to know is what's written on the horn which Belek of Beauval took from the hoard of the giant Faulhorn. Then I'll . . . leave you to get on with . . . whatever you were doing."

The ghosts exchanged glances. Not one spoke. Then, as one, they looked towards the high table. At the centre of the high table was the great throne of Mirasol, and on that throne sat the ghost of the last of Mirasol's kings— Belek. This ghost moved, now, within its heavy shadows and looked down at the girl who stood in the aisle between two of the long tables, holding up a lighted match.

"Who are you?" intoned the ghost, its voice thin and anguished.

Helen's flesh crept. She didn't mind. It was only a normal reflex action.

"Helen Hilversun," she said, and added: "if your majesty pleases."

The ghost-king bowed his head, very slightly. He turned, then, to point to the great horn, which hung on the wall behind the throne. His diamond-eyes looked first at the horn, then at Helen, and back and forth again.

Helen understood. Belek was under enchantment. He could not speak of the horn. There was something strange in the way he moved his eyes, and the expression on his face. Ghosts do not have a great capacity for expression, and are notorious for being unable to exercise strict control over their appearance. Belek was trying hard to indicate something, but Helen didn't know what.

The horn was brass, seven feet from end to end, and its mouth yawned fully three feet across. It was curved into a shallow arc, and it hung from the wall supported by two steel chains extended from brass rings welded to its body.

Helen walked down the aisle and around the high table. It was a bit of a squeeze getting past the chairs at the end of the rank. The great hall didn't seem so great with a crowd like this crammed into it. When she eventually stood before the horn she could see by the light of the match that two words had been graven into the metal about halfway along its length.

They were: BLOW HARD.

"Is that all?" muttered Helen. "All this fuss just for *that*. I could have guessed *that*."

She spoke aloud, temporarily unmindful of the gathered throng. Then she remembered, and turned away guiltily.

Every glittering eye was fixed upon her face.

"I'm sorry," she said. "I . . . think I'd better go now."

She took one step.

Then she hesitated.

There was something about those glittering eyes. The ghosts looked utterly forlorn . . . desperate . . . tormented.

Their faces suggested greater, deeper pain than mere flesh could ever know. With ghosts, this is not unusual. But Helen felt an urgency about the way these ghosts looked that was strange. She knew that they wanted to say something, but they couldn't. A calculated supernatural force was stopping them.

Inspiration struck her.

She walked over to the ghostly courtier who sat at the right hand of the king.

"Excuse me," she said. "May I borrow your chair?"

The ghost stood up and bowed.

It was quite a heavy chair—nothing like the throne of course, but still an impressive piece of furniture. Helen had to put the match down, jamming it into a crack where the upholstery was imperfect. Then she dragged the chair over to the wall, using both hands. She set it beneath the mouthpiece of the horn, and climbed up. She couldn't shift the horn far, but found that she could swing the mouthpiece away from the wall sufficiently to allow her to set her mouth to it.

She blew.

Her breath was swallowed up by the horn. Nothing happened.

She blew harder. No sound issued from the horn.

She blew as hard as she possibly could, and still nothing happened. The horn drank her breath without the slightest difficulty.

Helen turned back to the ghostly assembly, and said: "I can't do it. I'm sorry, but I just can't do it."

Written on their faces was an anguish more terrible than anything Helen had ever seen. It was worse than anything her imagination could have conjured. It defied description.

She turned to the horn again, and looked hard at the

mouthpiece. It was just a circle of brass—meant for a giant's lips and lungs, no doubt, but still only a circlet of brass. She knew that she couldn't work any magic on the horn—that was out of the question. But perhaps . . .

She didn't mutter this spell, but spoke it loud and clear, careful of the pronunciation.

"Breath, breath, come and blow, help me now a wind to sow; wind into the horn must flow, sound a good note, high or low."

Then she blew, hard.

And harder.

As hard as she could.

And still harder . . .

And from the mouth of the horn came the merest trace of sound—a thin, low-pitched whisper like the sound guitar strings make when the wind touches them.

Helen took her lips from the mouthpiece, but the sound went on. It grew in volume and rose in pitch, changed from a whisper to a cry, from a cry to a scream, from a scream to an almighty roar. . . .

Helen leapt down, clapping her hands to her ears, and ran, not pausing to pick up the match or return the chair or even to go round the high table—she dived straight under it and came up in the aisle on the other side, and ran pell-mell for the oaken door, which still stood ajar.

The note grew, from a roar to a howl, from a howl to a boom that must surely have vibrated the Earth itself. . . .

As she reached the doorway the note reached its climax, which was a sound too big to be described, a thunder *outside* the Earth. . . .

With the thunderclap came a bolt of lightning, arrowing out of the boiling blue-black sky, not aimed at the tall towers of Mirasol's keep but deep into the courtyard, hurtling deep into the encaged darkness to strike with astonishing violence the weathervane atop the old well. In striking home the searing white light of the electric bolt stripped away the shadows with an awesome flourish.

Following the lightning came the rain, in a mighty torrent, which washed the walls and the stairs and the floor of the courtyard free of the slimy dust of centuries.

Helen looked back and saw that the great hall was quite deserted. Belek of Beauval and his ghostly court were released from their enchanted bondage, gone to eternal rest. Even the moaning from beneath was gone, still forever.

When she looked back into the yard again, Helen saw the strange lumps which scattered the flagstones regain their colour and their form and their life. They became small coloured birds: goldcrests, bullfinches, yellowhammers, robins, bluebirds and bulbuls. They fluttered up into the rain-filled sky, too buoyant with freedom to heed the great cascade, and they flew away.

My dear Prince Damian,
   (began the letter)
   The words engraved upon the horn of the giant Faulhorn, which hangs in the Great Hall of Castle Mirasol, are: BLOW HARD.
   Your second task, as you doubtless already know, is to discover the name of the lamia who guards the forbidden city. I would wish you luck, but I am sure that you do not need it. I look forward to receiving your answer.

With best wishes,
Helen

"It doesn't seem quite so easy," admitted Ewan. He was not just facing Coronado, but also the king and the prince. As soon as the letter arrived he had been invited along to the council chamber to discuss the matter.

"You can't do it," said the king.

Ewan shrugged. "I won't know that until I've tried, will I?"

"I won't have it!" said the king. "I'm going to put a stop to this whole silly affair. Sending Damian off to the enchanted forest and the ruins of Ora Lamae . . . They're just about the most dangerous places in the world. Who does this girl think she is? I simply will not have it. Asking my son to risk his very life. . . ."

Coronado coughed, politely. The king hesitated. "Well," he said, "she *thinks* it's Damian that's doing it. And anyhow, this boy's one of my subjects, and in his way is just as dear to me as my son. So there!"

Coronado shook his head. "That's not what I mean, sire," he said. "The thing is that we don't actually know how hard these questions seem to the young lady. To an enchanter's daughter they may seem to be mere riddles. Perhaps she obtains the answers by magical means— crystal gazing or some other manner of divination—and expects us to do the same. We don't know that she actually intends anyone to go to these places."

"We haven't got any crystal balls," said the king, testily. "Or any other of the divi-things you were talking about. And it's all irrelevant. I'm going to put a stop to it, and that's that. It's unfair!"

"It certainly is," put in the prince. "I don't think we should have anything more to do with these people. Let them rot in their creepy castle. Keep civilization for the civilized, *I* say."

"Your majesty is reconciled, then," said the prime minister in falsely honeyed tones, "to the ruin of his dynasty . . . and very probably of Caramorn itself."

"There are other ways," snapped the king, with an airy wave of his hand.

"Name three," Coronado snapped back.

"Don't you talk to me like that!" said the king. "Or I'll . . ."

While Rufus Malagig IV paused for thought concerning the nature of the appropriate threat, Coronado interrupted. "Never mind," he said, calmly. "Your majesty will please accept my resignation. I'll collect my belongings and be gone by nightfall."

The king's jaw dropped, and he stared with open amazement at his ex-prime minister.

"You can't do that!" he said.

"I have," answered Coronado.

"You can't just *leave* me. This is your mess as well as mine, and I *demand* that you stay and find a way out of it. It's your duty. You don't catch me backing down on my responsibilities, do you?"

"I don't know, sire," said Coronado. "Are you prepared to follow this through, then? Or are you still intent on putting a stop to it?"

The king's face turned crimson. "That's not what I meant!" he shouted.

"It's what *I* mean," answered Coronado, his voice still deathly calm. "This may be a dangerous game, but it's the only game left to us. And if your majesty will forgive me pointing it out, Damian is not at risk. Ewan is the one who will take any risks there are to be taken. He does so, I might add, against my own advice. I suggested that we should bluff it out, and I still think that might be best. But while he's willing to add to our chances of winning through, I'm willing to accept his help. I'd be failing in my duty if I didn't. I think he's a fool to do it—but if he's willing, I can't say no. And I can't let you say no, either."

The king subsided, and so did Coronado. Rufus Malagig IV glanced at his son, and then stared very hard at Ewan.

"You're actually prepared to go to the Forbidden City?" he asked. "To hunt for a lamia?"

"Yes," answered Ewan.

"Why? For heaven's sake, why?"

Ewan bit his lower lip, and furrowed his brow. "I'm not sure that I can explain it to you," he said. "But it seems to me that I'm somehow *committed*. Ever since . . . well, I went to the enchanted forest because I thought it would be fairly easy. It wasn't. But after what happened there . . . I don't know how or why . . . but something turned me around in time. It took me back the best part of a day, so I wouldn't be late with the answer. And it's as though it has tied a knot in my lifeline. And bound up in that knot—I don't know how or why—is . . . not a compulsion exactly, but. . . ."

The king's gaze flicked abruptly back to Coronado.

"You know what this means?"

"I know," said the prime minister.

"*I* don't!" complained Damian.

"It's an enchantment," said the king. "Someone's put a spell on him. And if it's on him, it's on this whole business."

"I don't think we can back out," said Coronado. "Whether we do or not, Ewan is going to the Forbidden City. Whether we involve ourselves or not, he'll get the answer to the question . . . or fail in the attempt. I'm afraid that the set of verses lurking in your library, sire, is a piece of magic . . . and it's still active, even after all these years."

Damian looked sideways at Ewan and edged away from him. He didn't like the idea of standing next to persons afflicted with curses.

"I don't like this," said the king. "I don't like *any* of it."

"Nor do I," said Coronado. "But there's one thing we mustn't overlook."

"What?" asked the king.

"If we carry on, it might just work. We *could* end up with a royal marriage and a saved kingdom."

Ewan coughed politely. Coronado looked at him questioningly.

"I understand your preoccupation with the political aspects of the problem," said the boy, "but it seems to me that there's something else that might warrant thinking about."

"Which is?" prompted the prime minister.

"Just supposing," said Ewan, "for the sake of argument, that we manage to get through the whole set of six questions—thus, of course, fulfilling the requirements of the bargain—we will then have completed the spell. What I want to know is what will happen *then?* What's the spell *for?* What does it *do?* So far it appears to have disenchanted Methwold forest—and I suspect it may have had the same effect on the haunted castle—and perhaps the second verse has similarly limited objectives. But the third verse is different . . . and I believe that it all forms a coherent whole, in any case.

"We've begun to work out the pattern—all right, we carry on. We complete it. But what happens next?"

Coronado and the king looked at one another grimly. Prince Damian shook his head. It was a very good question. And nobody had an answer.

In the meantime, Helen's thoughts were just as confused and uncertain. She, too, was a prisoner of the pattern that had now been established. She had a memory, though a vague one, of the conversation with the image in the mirror. She could not quite remember what had been said, but the three verses of the last will and testament of Jeahawn Kambalba were burned into her mind.

Although Ewan had the facilities of the palace library at his disposal it was Helen who was in a better position to know what kind of thing she had become involved in. Ewan could look up the biographical details of Jeahawn Kambalba's career, but Helen knew what some of those details meant.

Jeahawn Kambalba had ended the wars of enchantment that might otherwise have been deadlocked for a thousand years. Through curse and countercurse, barrier and blockade, illusion and dimension he had battled his way to the core of each source of the magical blights that lay upon the land. Had any two of the four great mages—Elfspin, Viranian, Ambrael and Jargold—truly combined their powers they could have defeated him, but although there were notional alliances and agreements and treaties, each of the four mistrusted his allies as much as his enemies. One of the four had been utterly destroyed, one stripped of his powers. The other two were brought before a court and consigned to eternal prisons. The wars had ended. The one thing Jeahawn had not managed to accomplish was to undo any significant portion of the damage which the four and their many allies (human and inhuman) had done to the land itself. That kind of power could not be summoned instantaneously, but had to build over a period of time.

A spell, left to its own devices for a century or more, fed with energy from without the Earth, might gather such power. It could be supervised from beyond the material world, where Jeahawn's ghost still operated though he was long dead. But the *implementation* of such a spell—the working of its rituals and the acceptance of its dictates—could only be done within the world, by living agents appropriate to the task.

This, Helen knew, was the greater purpose, which had ensnared her. She and one other—Prince Damian, as she believed—had been adopted by the spell as its arms and legs, its heads and hearts.

Where would it end . . . if it ended at all?

She knew no more than Ewan and Coronado. The last verse was as enigmatic to her as to them. Only one person might know what that verse signified, and that was Sirion Hilversun. And she could not ask him. She was ashamed of the fact that she could not, because she only half realized that it was a part of the obligation which Jeahawn had put upon her. We are all selfish with our troubles and fears, as we often are with our hopes and ambitions, and it is natural to feel a little uncomfortable in the presence of such selfishness, whether it is magically ordained or not.

Apart from this misery there was, in Helen, a deep and profound fear, for she understood—as Ewan did not—that the fulfilment of a spell such as this might easily involve the destruction of its pawns. As an enchanter's daughter she knew the terrible price which powerful magics often exact. A spell of this power might require of its participants not only courage, enterprise and strength, but pain and terror . . . and even death. Magic feeds gluttonously on *all* the emotions, both positive and negative, and takes its power as much from the dark side of life as the bright.

Jeahawn himself was long gone—consumed by his own parasitic enchantments, eaten up by his own powers. But for those who inherited his legacy there might be a similar fate, and perhaps an even less kindly one.

Helen knew the danger implicit in the Arts magical. She also knew that Damian did not. The one thing that she was sure of beyond all possible doubt was the fact that it would be much worse for all concerned if the spell, once started, were to fail than if it were to succeed.

She did not like Price Damian. She did not want to marry him. But she had seen what had happened to Castle Mirasol, and had deduced what had happened to Methwold forest, and she had worked out the implications of these events. Given a day to think before she had had to send her answer to Jessamy she had realized how childish and how unimportant her earlier attitude had been. Bearing all this in mind, she resolved that at the due time she would go to the Forbidden City of Ora Lamae herself, to see how the prince would cope with the dreaded lamia—and, if necessary, to help.

It was well past midnight when Ewan put his pen down for the last time. He hadn't intended to work so late, but he had known all day that the end was in sight, and he had felt obliged to see it through.

He had finished cataloguing the library. All that he had to do now was send the catalogue to Heliopolis, where the archivists would look it over, fix a price, and—if necessary—delegate one of their number to come and sort out any final queries before drawing up an agreement. There was unlikely to be much haggling. The university knew perfectly well that Rufus Malagig IV had to sell and would only offer what the books were worth so as not to prejudice their reputation for fair dealing (not everyone who sold books to them was in a state of desperation).

All in all, Ewan felt well satisfied as he climbed down from his stool. He had a strong suspicion that if he had done the work well the university would take him back even in the absence of a government grant. He thought

that all would be well even if the prince *didn't* win his
bride—always provided, of course, that he could survive
his two further ordeals at the World's Edge.

He picked up the candle from the shelf where it had
stood in order to illuminate his work. He began to make
his way between the bookshelves, with little thought in
his head except how tired he was. As he turned a corner,
however, he became aware that his candle wasn't the
only light in the room. Just inside the door, apparently
waiting for him, was a shape cut out of the shadow by
an odd kind of silvery haze. The haze had the form of
a man—a small man with a little goatee beard and an
oddly childlike face.

Ewan stopped dead, staring at the ghost.

The ghost seemed to fade a little under the stare. In
the candle's light the shape blurred.

"I'm sorry," said the ghost. "I'm *trying* to get a better
manifestation, but it's not easy. I've never been here
before."

"Really?" said Ewan. There was a slight quaver in
his voice. "You know, I never quite believed in ghosts
until this moment."

"*That* doesn't help much, either," said the ghost.
"Scepticism is so demoralizing. Couldn't you try harder?
It's in your own interests."

"Oh," said Ewan, faintly. "I believe *now*. In fact,
unless I wake up in the morning thinking this is a dream,
I don't suppose I'll ever doubt again."

"Promises, promises..." muttered the ghost, trying
hard to get himself back into focus. Finally, he managed
it, and the rounded face reappeared, every hair in the
goatee perfectly formed.

"Have you come to haunt me?" asked Ewan.

"Why?" asked the spectre. "What have you done?

Oh, never mind . . . just a joke. I'm not *that* kind of ghost. In fact, I'd rather you didn't use the word 'ghost' at all. Personally, I think it's rather vulgar. I'd rather be thought of as an apparition, or if you really must, as a phantasm. Spelt with a P-H, of course—only the snobs use an F. Anyhow, no terrible moans, no atmospherics, and I promise not to let my watch-chain clank. The voice is hollow, but I can't help *that* in *my* condition. I've come to help you, not to haunt you."

"Oh," said Ewan, utterly at a loss for words. The prickling sensation that was running up and down his spine refused to yield to these assurances.

"My name," said the apparition, "is Wynkyn. *Please* don't bother with the usual jokes, or even the unusual ones. I've heard them all before, and I don't doubt that it's my fate to go on hearing them through all eternity. Let's skip them just this once. I've from the Vaults Beyond."

"Beyond where?" asked Ewan, feeling that he ought to say *something*.

"Beyond *here*, of course," replied Wynkyn. "Where else?"

Ewan shook his head and shrugged his shoulders. He was most uncomfortable.

"The thing is," said the apparition, "that you're entitled to a little help on the second verse. It's the hard one, you see, where you have to deal with creatures which are . . . well, not to put too fine a point on it . . . rather nasty. Inimical, one might say, always assuming that one knew what the word meant. Did I tell you that I was a poet when I was alive? Still am, in a way . . . Where was I?"

"Inimical," said Ewan, obligingly.

"Oh, yes," said Wynkyn. "The lamia and the monster.

Not nice. Kill you as soon as look at you. So you're entitled to a little protection. Jeahawn put a codicil on the will, you see. . . . It's not in the short version, but it's in the original which is on file in the Vaults. . . ."

"Hang on," said Ewan, who felt decidedly weak at the knees. "Do you mind if I sit down?"

"Not at all," said the apparition. "I'll stand, if you don't mind. Sedentary job, you know. And besides which, it's easier to stay in focus while in the upright posture— it says so in the manifestation handbook."

Ewan sat down on a convenient heap of out-of-date grimoires, and leaned back on a shelf loaded with al-chemical journals. They felt reassuringly solid.

"I say," said Wynkyn, holding up his hand. "I'm getting brighter. The last little bits of your doubt must have disappeared. You believe in me now, all right."

"Well," said Ewan, feeling slightly better now, "I'm an open-minded sort of a chap. Always ready to believe the evidence of my eyes."

"I wouldn't go quite *that* far," said the apparition. "I've seen some things *nobody* could believe. But no matter. The thing is, do you understand what I've told you?"

"In a word," said Ewan, "no."

The apparition clicked his insubstantial tongue. "Oh, dear," he said. "All right, let's start again. Slowly. My name's Wynkyn. Please don't bother with the jokes. . . ."

"All right," Ewan intervened. "I got *that* bit. You're name's Wynkyn, it isn't funny, and you're a friend of Jeahawn the Judge, right?"

Wynkyn shuddered slightly, losing his focus momentarily. "No, no, no," he said. "I'm just a civil servant. I've nothing to do with enchanters and that sort of thing. I work in the Vaults Beyond."

"What are the Vaults Beyond?" asked Ewan, feeling quite lost.

"The Vaults Beyond are the offices of the Supernatural Bureaucracy."

"I was afraid you were going to say something like that," said Ewan, with a slight groan. "Look, I'm tired. Do you think you could *explain?* Carefully?"

"You *are* a dull one," complained the apparition. "It's very simple. You don't think that magic just works by itself, do you? Records have to be kept. Spells don't just work . . . they have to go through channels. Who do you think keeps all the curses that were ever laid on file? Who do you think sees to it that whenever the conditions of a curse are transgressed the transgressor suffers the effects of the curse? Who do you think keeps accounts of all the things that are conjured up by wizards, and balances out the conjurations by subtracting the objects elsewhere? Do you have *any* idea *at all* of the *colossal* amount of paperwork that goes into the business of keeping magic working?"

"I didn't realize . . ." said Ewan.

"Of *course* you didn't realize," said the apparition, who was by now quite incensed. "No one gives a thought to us! Every spell registered, every curse on file, every magical object, its properties and penalties, properly classified. Oh, yes, you think a lot of enchanters reciting their silly rhymes and getting a result with a flash and a bang—but you never think at all about the poor clerks working behind the scenes to make sure the spell works properly, or even at all, and balancing out the books, and keeping an accurate record. We make occasional mistakes, I know, but we're only superhuman. . . . Nobody understands, all we get is insults and jokes, insults and jokes. . . ."

Ewan coughed. "I think I understand now," he said.

"Oh," said Wynkyn, calming down. "Oh, well ... that's all right. You understand. I'm just a messenger. Jeahawn Kambalba's will has a codicil, and I'm here to carry out its dictates. Just doing an honest job, working my way toward the Eternal Reward."

"What's the Eternal Reward?" asked Ewan. He tried to stop himself, but he was too late, and nearly bit his tongue. But Wynkyn didn't immediately launch into another tirade.

"It's what you go on to when you've done your stint," he said. "Nobody knows what it's really like, but we all look forward to it. We reckon that there's probably a whole series of different ones for people with different ideas. We talk about it a lot during our tea breaks. Mostly we think it ought to be a kind of summery, pastoral place, although one or two of us would like a little more action. We have one fellow who reckons the Eternal Reward is a castle where everyone spends all their time eating, drinking and fighting, and another who thinks it's a perpetual round of dressing up in funny clothes and hunting little brown animals with packs of dogs. You get all sorts in the Vaults, I can tell you ... or, rather, I can't, because I've got work to do. There's a big flap on right now, you see—not much going on this side but a proper blitz in the Vaults, getting everything tidy and all sorted out, everything in its file and the like, triple-checking the records and auditing the accounts. Rumor has it we're packing up the whole operation soon and *all* going to our Eternal Reward at once, but that's just wishful thinking, if you ask me. I think it's just a routine panic."

"Yes," said Ewan, quickly. "I see. Perfectly. So, if you could just give me the message, or whatever...."

"Ah!" said Wynkyn. "Glad you reminded me. That's

what I came here for, isn't it?"

The apparition reached a spectral hand into the blackness of the deep shadow which surrounded him, and drew out a ghostly guitar. He placed it on the floor, where it gleamed whitely. Ewan reached out to touch it, but his hand went straight through it, and he recoiled quickly.

"Wait a minute," said Wynkyn, crossly. "Hold your horses. Don't rush me. There's a spell that goes with it, if I can just . . . oh, yes. . . . *Pluck the strings and play a tune, soft and subtle, sweet and slow; watch her dance and hear her croon, she'll whisper the name you need to know*."

The guitar became solid.

"Well," said Wynkyn. "It worked. Though I can't say I think much of the rhyme. Pure doggerel, you know. I can't think why they call magic an art. No *real* poet would write silly jingles like that. More suited to the advertising industry, if you ask me."

Ewan reached out again to touch the guitar. This time he managed it. It was ordinary wood, slightly cold to the touch.

"Had to get special powers to do that, you know," said the apparition. "Three different forms to fill in."

Ewan picked up the guitar and touched the fibrous strings lightly. Then, reassured that it was quite real, he brought it into position and began to pick out the chords of "Baa, baa, black sheep."

"Oh, dear," said the watching apparition. "That's *terrible*. Can't you do better than that?"

"Can you?" retorted Ewan.

"That's not the point," said Wynkyn, sniffing. "The point is that you'll have to work extremely hard to keep the lamia dancing to *that*."

Ewan scowled and began to pick out a traditional

dance tune. The apparition raised his eyes disdainfully, and his gaze fell upon the serried ranks of books for the first time.

"I say!" he said. "This is a library!"

Ewan sat the guitar aside.

"What did you think it was?" he asked, nastily. "One of your precious filing cabinets?" He was a little hurt by the derisory references to his guitar playing.

Wynkyn ignored the sarcasm. "You don't suppose," he said, with a slight catch in his voice, "that they've got any of *my* books here. I'm a poet, you know... when I was alive."

"I've got a catalogue here," said Ewan, moving back into the darkness to take up his pile of parchment. "It's in alphabetical order. What's your surname?"

"Wilkinson," said the apparition. "Wynkyn Wilkinson. I was one of the esoteric school, you know."

Ewan flipped through the pages and found the appropriate one. "Wilkinson, Wynkyn," he read out. *"Synchronous Sonnets*, The Esoteric Press, undated. Spine rubbed, slight foxing. No dust wrapper. That's all."

Wynkyn released a long, hollow sigh of ecstasy. *"Synchronous Sonnets,"* he whispered. "Ah, youth! So long ago, and still remembered! Beloved by posterity!"

Ewan felt that it might be extremely undiplomatic to point out that none of the books in the library had been read for decades, and many of them had undoubtedly never been read at all.

"I suppose," said the apparition, dreamily, "that this in itself is a form of Eternal Reward. My work survives! O joy! O rapture!"

And so saying, the emissary from the Vaults Beyond faded out.

Only the candlelight remained... and the guitar.

Ewan picked up the guitar and tucked it under his arm. He made as if to open the door, and then had an afterthought. Candle in hand he went back into the maze of shelves, and quickly located the book he sought: *Synchronous Sonnets,* by Wynkyn Wilkinson. He tucked that under his arm, too, and took it away to read in bed.

He had never met a *real* poet before. And he was never likely to run into another one who had been dead for several centuries.

{10}

HELEN WALKED ALONG the marbled pavement which shone blue and green in the afternoon sun. It was cold beneath her feet; she could feel the iciness even through her shoes. The blues and greens swirled together in all kinds of liquid patterns, and the pavement seemed like a frozen stream.

There was no dust in the Forbidden City. Like Castle Mirasol, Ora Lamae was a dead and haunted place, but in a very different fashion. Castle Mirasol had been condemned to age and decay and rot as it stood, but Ora Lamae seemed to have been simply *melted* into slag and re-solidified to the texture of petrified wood, crystallized for all eternity.

Once, Ora Lamae had been the pearl of World's Edge, a city of semi-precious stone. Every brick of every building had been carved with care and decorated. The streets had been covered by exotic metal strips over which magical cars might glide. The people, too, it was said, had been beautiful—clothed in many-coloured silks, with skins that were smooth and eyes as bright as sapphires. But that was long ago, or "once upon a time," as the stories had it.

Now. . . .

Spells of awesome power had long since crushed the mighty buildings with fists of fearsome heat, turned their hard lines soft and left them shapeless lumps. All the patterns of the city were blurred now, smudged and creased, all semblance of order lost.

Ora Lamae now held only the deformed ghosts of all its palaces and domes, arches and spires. Everything that the people had built, war and magic had obliterated, leaving only the mockery of ruins.

Huge black birds with bald heads gathered in the wreckage now—carrion birds which flew by night into the wider world but which hid by day, here, where no one would see them or care. The birds watched Helen as she walked the streets of the city, resentful of her presence. She ignored them.

Helen's was not the only unwanted presence disturbing the sanctuary of the vultures. She realized as much when she heard the music. At first, she could not make it out, but when she was closer she realized that it was someone playing a guitar. She had not heard music played since Sirion Hilversun's hands had become so stiff that it was painful for him to pluck the strings of his ancient harp. She herself had only ever learned to play the flute, not very well.

She recognized the tune that was being played as an old song which belonged by tradition to this part of the world—perhaps more to the magic lands than to Caramorn. She tried to recall the words but couldn't. They were lost in the forsaken memories of her childhood.

Ewan was concentrating hard. He had the feeling of the instrument by now, and he felt that despite Wynkyn's less-than-complimentary comments he wasn't doing too badly. He might not know many tunes, but he thought he could pick out a few competently enough, and the instrument seemed to be helping him. Though he hated to admit it, it was a much finer guitar than any his father had ever made.

It took him some time to realize that he was no longer alone. As soon as he noticed the girl, though, he stopped playing and put the instrument down.

"Hello," he said.

Helen was standing on a crude pedestal of once molten rock, which might have been a fountain or a pillar in days of old. She looked down at Ewan, who was sitting on the pavement resting his back against a blue-white lump that might have been almost anything. She frowned, wondering who on earth this could be, and not answering his greeting.

"Do you come here often?" asked Ewan, not sure whether it was a joke or not.

"No one comes here," she said. "Not ever."

Ewan shrugged. "That makes you the lamia," he said. "But you're not supposed to come out except at night. What it makes me, I'm not entirely sure."

Helen felt that this comment was slightly irreverent. But she was suddenly struck by the thought that perhaps it hadn't been Prince Damian who had disenchanted Methwold forest after all.

"Who are you?" she asked, bluntly.

"My name's Ewan," he replied. "*Are* you the lamia? If you'll pardon me saying so, you don't look like someone who lives on other people's blood."

"Of course I'm not the lamia," said Helen, brusquely.

"Ah, well," said Ewan, with fake sadness. "Never mind."

"What are you doing here?" asked Helen.

"Isn't it obvious? I'm waiting for the lamia."

"Why?"

"Oh," said Ewan, airily. "I've always thought that I ought to try and make new acquaintances, widen the circle of my friends . . . that sort of thing. Today seemed just right for making a start. And I don't know any lamias, so. . . ."

Helen knew that her mouth was hanging open in astonishment, but couldn't quite muster the energy to shut it. This was *too* much. She took a couple of minutes to muster her composure, during which time the boy gazed at her steadily.

"Well," she said, finally. "I'll wait with you. When the lamia turns up you can introduce me."

Ewan grinned. "I will," he promised. "Just as soon as I find out her name." He was still staring, but now Helen met his stare, and he quickly dropped his gaze, looking down at the guitar. He put out his hand and rippled the strings lightly.

"That's a beautiful guitar," said Helen, descending from her pedestal to stand beside him.

"True," said Ewan. "A present from a dead poet."

"A poet?"

"Well," said Ewan, remembering the verses he had read in the early hours of the morning, "that's *his* story."

"Who are you?" asked Helen, again.

"As I recall," said Ewan, "it was *you* who didn't answer the question. I'm Ewan, son of an instrument-maker in Jessamy, currently on vacation from the University of Heliopolis."

Helen said nothing.

"All right," said Ewan, "I'll tell you. You're Helen Hilversun, and you didn't believe the first answer, so you came to check up. And now you know that Prince Damian's sitting at home in the palace while other people run his errands. Right?"

Helen laughed. "Right," she agreed.

"How's Castle Mirasol?" asked Ewan.

"Clean as a new pin," replied Helen. She felt more comfortable, now. It seemed rather obvious now that she thought about it. Of *course* it hadn't been Damian who had disenchanted Methwold. "You're cheats," she added. "You and Damian both. This isn't fair."

"True," admitted Ewan. "I suppose you could say that all was not fair and above board. I guess you could call the whole thing off if you wanted to. *Do* you want to?"

"Are you talking about the marriage or the spell?"

"Both."

"I don't want to marry Damian, and I won't. But the spell. . . . I suppose you know that we can't stop now."

Ewan nodded. "I did have an inkling," he admitted.

"Why did you get involved?" asked Helen.

"The prime minister. He appealed to my sense of loyalty. He also applied a little gentle blackmail. I could have refused, but it would have been difficult . . . and I was a little bit fascinated by the whole thing. Why does anyone get involved with anything?"

"You were manipulated. By Jeahawn the Judge."

Ewan shrugged. "Maybe just a little bit," he said. "What difference does it make? He pushed us, we let him. We're in now. The question is: how do we get out?"

"You're either very brave," said Helen, "or you're an idiot."

"Actually," replied Ewan, "those are pretty much the same alternative conclusions I reached myself. Why don't you sit down. Dusk will fall soon. Then we'll see some action."

Helen sat down beside him. The pavement felt very cold, even through the thickness of her jeans.

"We'll have to see it through," she said.

"I guessed so," said Ewan.

"We could get ourselves killed," she added.

"Maybe," he replied. "But this thing is *intended* to go through. There are forces working for us as well as against us. I got the guitar last night, special delivery. It's the thing that's supposed to enable me to get the lamia to reveal her secret name. If I had to bet I'd say that you'll get a little something to help with this Zemmoul character. I presume you're acquainted with Fiora?"

"It's a waterfall," said Helen, glumly. "It falls into a bottomless pool. And in the pool..."

"...lives something pretty horrible. I see."

"It's a very *big* monster," said Helen.

"We can take him," Ewan assured her. "With a little help from Wynkyn."

"We?" queried Helen.

"Certainly," said Ewan. "It's not a competition any more. Or if it is, we're on the same side. Two of us together must stand a better chance at all stages of the pattern. Right?"

Helen looked at him, uneasily.

"Or were you thinking of going back to Moonmansion now?" he asked. "Now that you've checked up and found out the truth?"

She shook her head. "I'm staying," she said.

"Bravery?" he asked. "Or idiocy?"

"Who knows?"

Silence fell. Ewan picked up the guitar, laid it across his knee, and stroked the strings, just enough to bring forth a long, sweet note.

"What are Hamur and Sheal?" he asked.

"Gates," she replied. "Gates to nowhere. They stand above the limitless abyss. Sometimes, in the old days, things used to come through them. Terrible things. But not for many, many years."

"What about people going through from this side?"

"No one ever does," she told him. "And if they do . . ."

". . . they don't come back. This is a very predictable business, once you get into it. Isn't it?"

She didn't answer. After a pause, she said: "Do you think the will was intended just for us? Or might it have been anyone?"

"Anyone, I should think," said Ewan. "I'm no one special. Or perhaps it was intended for you and Prince Damian, and I'm just an unexpected substitute. I wonder if Damian can play the guitar?"

"Maybe," she said, "it selected us because we just happen to be the right people. The people who *can* do it."

There was a good deal of wishful thinking in this suggestion. But Ewan thought that they were both entitled to a little wishful thinking. He nodded optimistic agreement. Then he extended his hand towards her. She took it, and clasped it firmly. Then, with that agreement very much in mind, they waited quietly for dusk to fall.

Sirion Hilversun never usually worried overmuch about losing things. It often happened that he'd put something away and then forget where he'd find it. Usually, though, he'd remember as soon as it was time for him to stumble across it again. In addition, he could normally be sure that he *would,* when the time came, remember.

These days, however, he was perpetually lost in a

welter of confusion. He sat in his room while evening fell, lost in an endless maze of reminiscence which suddenly seemed so *empty,* realizing that he had virtually no consciousness of the future left at all.

"Everything," he thought, "is so dim and so dark. If only I'd kept a diary! Just a few minutes each night, before bed, writing down the principle events of the day to come. I'd have got into the habit. . . . I'd have been able to keep my memories disciplined. But no, I always had to muddle along, letting yesterday get mixed up with tomorrow, never knowing when I was up to, trusting to luck that I'd know when I was when I got then. If I had a diary to look back on I'd be able to sort out the shape of my life, find some sense and sequence. But as it is I'm just lost. Too old. Dying. I don't even know whether it's just that I can't remember the future or whether there isn't any future to remember. Perhaps the world's coming to an end, and I don't even know it. I don't remember dying . . . but I don't suppose people ever do. It's one of those things that always creeps up on you, is death. You never see it hiding nearby. I used to think that I might be young forever . . . even immortal. I suppose the day I began to remember growing old was the day I *started* growing old. What strange things memories are! How can you trust them, when they play such tricks . . . ?

As the thoughts slipped away, the silence that surrounded him became ominously obvious. The shadows cast by the evening sunlight that streamed through the window extended themselves slowly across the carpet.

"Helen . . ." he thought. "I must ask Helen. . . ."

But it was Helen that he had lost. She had gone out, without telling him where. And he couldn't, for the life of him, remember whether he'd ever see her again. . . .

{11}

EWAN DIDN'T SEE where the lamia came from. He looked up, and she was there—standing on the same mound where Helen had stood when he first noticed her.

It was dark now, but by no means pitch dark. Ewan had lit his lantern early, as a precaution, and Helen had worked a spell to make the candle burn long and bright, but the afterglow was still in the leaden, grey sky. It was the time of day which always seems still and quiet.

The lamia was tall, slender and graceful. She had hair that was long and straight, with a silvery sheen that was as pale as could be. She was dressed in a long silky robe, and that was silver, too. But she was certainly no ghost etched out of shadow. She was solid.

Her eyes had slit pupils like cats' eyes or snakes' eyes. The irises were green. Her face was finely shaped and very beautiful. When she saw Ewan looking at her, she smiled, and within her smile Ewan saw tiny pointed teeth and a forked tongue.

Ewan was ready with the guitar and laid his fingers instantly to the strings. Helen, too, had an instrument—Ewan's panpipes, which weren't much like a flute, but on which she had already learned to pick out a single simple dance tune. They began, not quite together, but the tunes soon met and merged.

The lamia glided from the pedestal of polished rock to the open space of the paving stones a little to one side. As she moved, the lamplight caught her eyes and made them glow like a tiger cat's. She was still smiling and hissing slightly. Her arms rose to the rhythm of the music, and her whole body began to sway and ripple. The song they played was an old one, whose notes were plaintive and slow. It had once had words that were replete with magic, but there were no words left now. Only the music. The music caught the lamia, turned her and swung her and swayed her in a gentle *pas seul*. She was still smiling, as though there was nothing in the world she liked better than to dance.

She was held captive within an area no more than a few strides in diameter, but within that invisible cage she moved with perfect freedom, with all the grace of a snake in water, a bird in slow motion, gliding around and around.

They played and played.

Night drew in—perhaps not as swiftly as they could have wished. Time seemed to be dragging, slowing down, and it seemed that they were set for a long wait. The afterglow vanished from the sky and the stars came out—feeble, twinkling stars that added little to the yellow glow of Ewan's lamp.

Not until the night was as dark as it ever could be, given that the stars were permitted to shine at all, did the *others* come.

They came as shadows, clothed in shadow. They were drawn to the music but shunned the light. They could not come forth to show themselves because they had no real forms to show. Like ghosts, they had no substance, but unlike ghosts they had no shape either, no inner glow to cut them out of the darkness. They were vague and amorphous in the very nature of their being—half-creatures that were half there and half not, half alive and half illusion.

They made a ring at the borders of the candlelight's reach. They gathered to watch the dance, prisoned by it as was the lamia, and they *joined* the dance—half hopping, half drifting round and around the rim of the circle of light.

"What are they?" whispered Ewan, making his voice so thin and frail that it would not break the rhythm of the dance.

Helen paused in her play to answer, in the same gentle tone: "Gaunts and ghasts and werethings. *Her* creatures, held in subjection to her. Creatures which haunt without being seen. They have no power . . . none at all, but are fearful nevertheless. The lamia drinks the blood, the black birds eat the flesh and the bones. These are all that remains."

It sounded, to Ewan, rather horrible, and almost beyond belief. They were, after all, only shadows—tricks of the light. But they were shadows in the imagination, too—tricks of thought and fear—and had to be dealt with. Courage would be a poor thing if it had only to face such things as are whole and solid.

Ewan's fingers never faltered now but found the notes with a sureness that came not from any innate talent and only partly from his long familiarity with musical instruments. The guitar itself was collaborating with him, alive in his hands, guiding him. Helen's accompaniment

on the panpipes was not really useful in the business of
making the lamia dance. But it was useful to Ewan—
there was a great reassurance in knowing that he was not
alone, that he was not working alone. There is really no
such thing as unnecessary help.

They played for an hour, and two . . . which seemed
like more. After that, they lost track of time altogether,
as it slowed down so much that they felt themselves
becalmed within a single moment. The stars stood still
in the sky, and the city of Ora Lamae was cut out from
the fabric of history, abstracted from the current of time
and isolated in a momentary cocoon.

Now (and everything more was *now*, and no other
time) the crowd at the edge of the candlelight grew no
more. The whole company was assembled in the slow,
sweet, sad dance. And the lamia began to croon her
wordless song.

Curiously, there was little *hissing* in the sound. It was
not at all the sound of a snake, It was, instead, a mellow,
gentle, *rounded* sound, whose notes flowed liquidly. It
blended with the music of the guitar, and seemed to have
much in common with it. Perhaps, indeed, it was a song
born of the guitar, and was being put into the lamia rather
than drawn out.

Either way, the lamia sang . . . and sang . . . and sang.

Ewan played while his fingers ached and their tips
were shot with pain. Helen played while her lips were
numb and her throat began to hurt. But they played and
played and didn't mind that the lamia danced so light
and free, not tiring at all, and sang without words or any
hint of a name escaping into the sound.

They played and played while Ewan wondered just
who was trapped and who—if anyone—was free. They
played and played while the dawn—the dawn that would
change the lamia back into a snake—did not come and

could not come. They played and played, in their tiny place outside of time.

Finally, Helen paused again—not resting this time, but stopping because neither her fingers nor her throat had the power to continue.

Ewan faltered.

"Ask her now!" whispered Helen. "Ask her name!"

Ewan came to his feet, slurring a note or two but not losing the rhythm of the dance, and recited:

> Where the towers of Ora Lamae stood
> a lamia waits to drink your blood—
> what secret name is in her bred?
> What secret name is in her bred?

The words mingled with the tune, and suddenly the forked tongue was writhing from the lamia's mouth, parting her lips and shaping the stream of liquid sound that spilled from her very being. It was not only the lamia that answered, but the shadowed host entranced at the fringes of the ring of light. A thousand half-voices joined, strained to their utmost, called out—and summoned up the merest whisper. So slight was their hold on half-life, so tenuous their half-being, that all as one they could only just make themselves heard.

Ewan's fingers lifted from the strings, but the strings continued on their own, not masking the chorus but adding to it, shaping the curling of the lamia's tongue, forming the syllables.

"Cas . . . *cor* . . . ia . . ." was the sound that came, as all the voices fused.

The music died, and the silence, so long deferred, seemed suddenly absolute.

The lamia, released, did not pause in her flowing movement, but came straight towards the boy, her arms held wide to embrace him.

The crowd, still and silent, watched.

Ewan knew now what was required. Names are power. In the naming of a night-creature there is the power of command.

"By the name of Cascoria," he said, his voice no more than slightly tremulous, "I command you to eternal rest."

The embrace was never sealed.

The candle in the lamp guttered and died.

Then the dawn came.

Later, Ewan and Helen managed to find a building which had not quite been rendered into a heap of slag. It still had a doorway and a couple of wrinkled windows. The hallway within was no longer square at any of its corners, and the walls were buckled, but it was shelter nevertheless.

It was raining—not the torrential rain that had scoured Mirasol, but a lazy, mild rain.

Both Ewan and Helen were utterly exhausted. They threw themselves on the polished floor. The grey mare, which had brought Ewan to the Forbidden City, was too tall and wide to come through the crumpled doorway, but was content to stand outside and get slightly wet.

"Well," said Ewan. "We did it."

"We certainly did," agreed Helen.

They sounded neither joyful nor triumphant, and this was not entirely due to their tiredness. They felt somehow *overcome* by the whole night's work. It had left them spiritually as well as physically exhausted.

"Those shadows..." whispered Ewan. "I never dreamed there could be so many."

"They aren't just innocent travellers picked off in Ora Lamae," said Helen. "Not, at any rate, since the city was destroyed. They're the victims of a thousand years, maybe more. A retinue gathered in all the places she's ever been."

Ewan shuddered and touched the wooden body of the guitar, gently—as though for reassurance.

"It's strange," he said. "When I turned the signpost round the whole of Methwold forest was transformed. But Ora Lamae didn't come back to life."

"Nor did Castle Mirasol," said Helen. "The rain washed it clean of old enchantments and the foul dirt that old enchantments gather, but it didn't mend the cracked stone. The ghosts went on to somewhere else—they didn't return to life. Only the birds came alive. Here, the lamia and her ghosts and gaunts are all gone, but the old palaces won't grow out of the wreckage, and the people in their coloured silks can't be recalled. These are ruins, built by men, destroyed by men . . . and ruins are ruins, whether magic helped to make them so or not. We can disenchant the natural, but the artificial can only be destroyed or remade."

"I see," said Ewan. And he did see. He was beginning to understand.

There was a pause—a languid, sleepy pause. It was finally interrupted by Ewan, who said: "What now?"

"Fiora," said Helen.

"I know that," answered Ewan. "But when? I don't like the way that time keeps jumping about. And we're entitled to some more help, I think. I need some sleep . . . and I think we ought to wait for Wynkyn, or whoever comes in his place. . . ."

"I should think so, too!" said a new voice, which Ewan recognized instantly as belonging to the ghostly poet.

He sat up, shaking off his tiredness. "Where are you?" he asked.

"I'm nowhere yet," complained the voice. "Really,

I'm expected to materialize in the most *awkward* places. It's daylight you know, and I've never been here before, and this shadow is definitely substandard."

"Move away from the door," said Helen to Ewan. Then, to Wynkyn: "I think we can get into one of the inner rooms, where there won't be as much light. This way."

She beckoned to Ewan, and they went through a doorway to the interior of the building, finding a room whose window had closed right up like a winking eye as the outer wall on that side had sagged terribly. The ceiling of the room slanted dramatically, but there was room to stand on the side that they went in, and some good, deep shadow caught in the mutilated angle of the walls.

The silver glow began to grow immediately, and Wynkyn managed—not without some difficulty—to shape himself and get into focus.

"That's better," he said.

"You didn't waste much time, did you?" asked Ewan.

"There isn't much time to waste," replied the apparition. "I'm on overtime, you know. I'm very sorry and all, but there simply isn't time for you to sleep out the day. The interference with time is strictly regulated, you know. You haven't actually moved back or forward at all . . . just stepped outside for a while. The night you saw from the clearing in Methwold was false night—an attribute of the forest itself. Anyhow, the powers-that-be think that Zemmoul has to be taken care of today, so that you can get to the third verse during tonight. It's something to do with the spell building up momentum, so that it has to move faster all the time, like a falling stone or a snowball rolling down a mountain. It's no good asking me to explain it—I'm a poet, and have no time for all that nasty mathematical, scientific stuff."

"We're very tired," said Ewan.

"Did anyone promise you it was going to be easy?" asked Wynkyn.

"No," admitted the boy.

"Then you've no grounds for complaint, have you?"

"Please," said Helen, "let's not bother with the arguments. The spell is building up power, that's all. You can't just *do* these things . . . you have to do them *right*. We understand."

The apparition gave her a tiny bow and a nice smile.

"Excellent," he said. "So let's get on. I'm afraid that the guitar has to come back, now."

Ewan opened his mouth as if to protest, but thought better of it, recognizing the inevitable. He looked back through the doorway, to the spot where he had abandoned the guitar, close to the outer door. It was already gone.

"However," the spectral poet went on, "there's a new present for the young lady. On temporary loan only, of course." So saying, he reached behind him into the thickest part of the shadow and slowly drew forth a sword with an ornate hilt and a long, glittering blade. It was still insubstantial, and glowed with the usual silvery light. Wynkyn laid it down on the floor. "Now what was that verse?" he muttered.

There was a long pause.

"Marvellous," commented Ewan. "A poet who can't remember a verse."

Wynkyn sniffed. "I never have any trouble with my own," he said. "But *I* write *real* poetry, not this stupid spell doggerel. *My* poetry has life, and wit and elegance and . . ."

"I read *Synchronous Sonnets* last night," said Ewan, coolly.

"Really!" said Wynkyn. "What did you think of it?"

"I think we ought to make a bargain," said Ewan. "You don't tell me what you think of my guitar playing, and I won't tell you what I think of your poetry."

Wynkyn winced. For a moment, he looked very hurt. Then he gathered himself together, drew himself up to his full (but rather inadequate) height, and said: *"Peasant!"*

"Thanks," said Ewan.

Helen kicked him on the ankle.

"I'm sure that it was excellent poetry," she said, "for those who have sufficient poetry in them to respond to it. But for the moment, we still need a doggerel verse to materialize the sword."

Wynkyn beamed at her. "It's a great pleasure," he said, "to find someone who understands. For you, my dear—it is, after all, *your* sword—I shall be able to recall the verse. . . . I have it now!"

"About time," muttered Ewan.

Wynkyn pointedly ignored him. He chanted:

"Zemmoul comes to take a lure, which motionless must lie; strike but once and strike him sure, above the baleful eye."

The sword solidified. Its hilt darkened through pale blue to indigo, and finally to ebony black. The blade remained silver but lost its glow.

"And I hope you like *your* part," said Wynkyn to Ewan, with rather more than the usual gleam in his eye, before he began to slowly fade out.

Helen knelt to pick up the sword, while Ewan frowned.

"What did he mean?" he asked.

Helen was testing the weight of the sword, and finding—much to her surprise—that it was light and comfortable in her two-handed grip. She didn't answer.

Ewan let the spell-rhythm run through his head again,

and an awful suspicion dawned on him.

"How big is this monster?" he asked.

"Very," she replied.

"And what does it eat?"

"For preference," she said, "people. But I suppose it doesn't get many these days and has to live on mud."

"So . . . er . . . what kind of bait are we supposed to use to tempt him out of his bottomless pool? What's the lure mentioned in the spell?"

She thought about it for a moment or two, and then the same answer occurred to her.

It was too dark for them to exchange glances where they stood, but Ewan was looking hard at where Helen was standing, and he imagined that she was doing likewise.

"Oh, well," said Ewan. "I suppose yours is the difficult bit. All *I* have to do is lie still."

❧{12}❧

WHEN THERE WAS no answer to his knock, Sirion Hilversun entered his daughter's bedroom. It was as he
thought. The bed had not been slept in.

"Oh, dear," he said, aloud. "Oh, dear. Where...."

He crossed the room to the dressing table, looking
around for some evidence of where Helen might have
gone, or why. Everything was neat and orderly, and quite
unhelpful. He was about to turn round and go out again
when he saw that the top left-hand drawer was not quite
closed. Although this did not seem particularly odd or
significant he reached out and opened it a little further.

Inside, there was an envelope. It had been opened,
but the letter had been shoved back inside. He recognized
it as the letter which had come from the palace a few
days before—the letter containing Prince Damian's first
question. The enchanter took the folded sheet of paper
out of the envelope, and opened it.

• • •

My dearest Helen,
    he read.

    The words written upon the stone beneath the signpost at the heart of Methwold forest were: TURN THE SIGNPOST ROUND.

    Then he skipped to:
on Faulhorn's horn . . . in Mirasol's haunted banquet hall?

He didn't bother with the rest.

"Mirasol?" he said to himself, softly. "She went to Mirasol. But she came back. It was the next day. . . ."

Then the thoughts began to strike him like the strokes of a tolling bell.

Methwold forest . . . turn the signpost round . . . disenchanted. Mirasol's banquet hall . . . the giant's horn. . . .

"Oh, no," murmured Sirion Hilversun, realizing what the juxtaposition of these things signified. "Oh, no! Not the will. . . . Jeahawn Kambalba. . . ."

The enchanter's face went as white as the paper he held in his trembling fingers. He looked up and saw his reflection in the magic mirror, staring at him with wide eyes.

"Where is she?" he whispered.

"You have to say: 'Mirror, mirror, on the wall,'" said the mirror. "It's in the rules."

"Where is she!" yelled the enchanter, at the top of his voice.

"All right, all right," said the mirror. "I didn't realize you felt like that. I don't know. I'm only her mirror."

"Don't take that tone with me, you lousebound looking-glass!" howled Sirion Hilversun. "When I ask you a question you give me an answer, you hear!"

The mirror quailed in its frame, distorting the image of the enraged enchanter horribly.

"I'm sorry!" it wailed. "I don't know, I tell you. Ever since that interference a few days ago I haven't been able to keep track of her."

"What interference?" asked the enchanter, icily.

"Didn't she tell you? I'm sure I don't know. We were talking quite amicably about difficult questions and all of a sudden I came over all peculiar. Overridden by another channel, if you ask me. *I* don't know what went on—I went out like a light. Had a headache ever since. Proper poorly, I've been."

"You . . ." hissed the enchanter, pausing as words failed him and lifting his fist in a gesture of furious menace.

"It's my duty to warn you," babbled the mirror, "that breaking me carries an automatic fine of seven years' bad luck. Calm down, please."

"Give me one good reason why I shouldn't smash you into little pieces," commanded the enchanter.

"Hold on," blustered the mirror. "Just hold on a minute. Wait . . . on reflection, it seems to me that perhaps I might be able to help you after all. *On reflection. . . ."*

The mirror paused to giggle at its unconscious pun. It was not a diplomatic moment. The enchanter raised his arm still higher.

"Waitwaitwait . . ." gurgled the mirror. "I saw her writing the reply. I couldn't help reading it . . . well, it was reflected in me, wasn't it? It wasn't as if I peeked. . . . And she asked something about a lamia in Ora Lamae."

"I *know* that," said Sirion Hilversun. "That's the second verse of the will. That doesn't help at all."

"But don't you see?" said the mirror, urgently. "That must be where she went. To check up on the prince, in case he was cheating. She went to Ora Lamae and heaven only knows what happened. . . . Maybe the lamia got them both. . . . *Don't hit me!*"

But Sirion Hilversun lost control at the suggestion that Helen might have been taken by the lamia. One of his fingers spat lightning, and the mirror shattered in its frame. As the pieces tinkled on the tabletop they chattered: "Seven years . . ."

"Don't you threaten *me*," murmured the enchanter, as his wild anger ebbed quickly away, draining out of him like water from a leaky bucket. "You couldn't force bad luck on me if you were the great mirror of the sea itself."

His fingers crushed the letter that he held into a ball, and he dropped it on to the shards of the mirror. He turned, and strode from the room with a purpose that his ancient legs had not found in forty years.

"Amnesia or no amnesia," he said, "I'm not dead yet. Not by a long way. Caramorn will regret this! If I don't get my daughter back I'll curse that land for a thousand years . . . and turn their precious prince into a slime-mould!"

It was late afternoon when Ewan and Helen reached Fiora. They had ridden the grey mare together—as neither of them was overweight the horse had not been seriously inconvenienced, and they had not asked more of her than a steady walk.

The waterfall tumbled from the heights of a great craggy cliff that lay between the precipitous mountains of southern Caramorn and the lands of World's Edge. The water fell into a great pool nearly a quarter of a mile across. But while the water that cascaded down was white and clean, the pool itself was all but black. Save for the place where the fall hit the surface, the pool was unnaturally still, the ripples that spread from the cascade moving slowly and quickly being damped and extinguished as they escaped the turbulence. The pool seemed to contain a thin, foul mud rather than pure water.

At the pool's further rim the outflow was a slow-running deep stream, which ran away across the magic lands to the edge of the world itself.

"The stream is gobbled up by the Great Grey Chaos that girdles the world," said Helen. "The water is dissipated into the mists that always envelope the edge itself. It used to be said that all the fresh, clean rain that falls from the sky all over the world is gathered and delivered here into this black pit, where the body of Zemmoul turns it foul. But I don't believe that. The world is so big, and so much rain falls. Once, so legend has it, there were many more things like Zemmoul—Chaos creatures that haunted every sea and lake, krakens and great sea-worms, jelly things with a million tentacles. Sometimes, in the *very* old times, some of them—especially the seaworms and the hippocampi—could assume the forms of men or horses, and come ashore riding the breakers on stormy days."

"You know some delightful stories," said Ewan, dismounting from the mare. As he released the reins he winced slightly.

"What's the matter?" asked Helen.

"Sore fingers," he said, with a wry grin. "Too much guitar playing." He reached for the knot by which Helen had tied the sword to the saddle, but she pushed his hand away and quickly worked it loose with her own fingers.

"I'll see what I can do," she said. "I'm not much of an enchantress, but sore fingers shouldn't be difficult."

"It's nothing," said Ewan.

But she took his hand in hers, and said: "Hold still." Then she chanted: *"Bruises fade and cuts seal, strength return and flesh heal."*

But nothing happened. The weals on Ewan's fingertips, and the swellings around the knuckle-joints, would not yield.

"Healing power and magic true," Helen tried again, *"make these hands as good as new."*

But that didn't work either.

"The cuts were made by magic strings," said Ewan. "Perhaps they can't be undone so easily. They'll heal, in their own time. Not to worry."

Helen did worry. She knew the wounds weren't serious—but they were wounds nevertheless, a penalty exacted by the spell of which they were the instruments. There might yet be more. She looked, uncomfortably, at her own hands, which had gripped the hilt of the sword. They were unscathed—so far.

"Look!" said Ewan, pointing.

Helen's heart skipped a beat. But it wasn't Zemmoul, rising already. Ewan was pointing to a weathered wooden post to which were attached two rusty shackles. It was close to the edge of the pool, about equidistant from the falls and the outflow.

"No prizes for guessing what that's for," said Ewan, dryly.

"Before the war," said Helen, "people lived in the woods close by. They didn't want Zemmoul coming out on hunting expeditions, so . . ."

"They used to keep him fed," Ewan finished. "I know the theory. Young girls, I suppose."

"Actually, no," said Helen. "It was a matriarchal society. And besides which, it's said Zemmoul preferred. . . ."

"All right," Ewan interrupted. "I get the idea. The whole picture. That's why I'm the bait."

Helen shrugged. "The luck of the draw," she said. "There are monsters and monsters."

"We'd better make a move," said Ewan. "Wynkyn seemed to think that we oughtn't to waste time now." So saying, he went over to the weathered post and sat down. Helen followed him and tried to fit one of the shackles around his foot. The locking mechanism was rusted away entirely, though, and it wouldn't close.

"I don't think we need bother," said Ewan. "I'll just pretend I'm nicely secured—just to reassure the monster that all's well. How big did you say he was?"

"Very," said Helen. "Can't say exactly. No one's clapped eyes on him for more than a hundred years."

"If it's that long since he last had his favourite food," muttered Ewan, "he's going to be very, very hungry."

"Think how delighted he'll be to see you. Isn't it nice to be popular?"

Ewan smiled weakly.

Helen moved back a step, looked at Ewan carefully, as if trying to decide whether the monster would think him a tasty enough morsel, and waved the sword experimentally.

"I'll be behind this rock," she said, pointing at a boulder some eight or ten feet away from the post.

"It's rather a long way, isn't it?" he answered, nervously.

"I'm very quick on my feet," she assured him. "And Zemmoul's reputed to be a trifle sluggish."

Ewan watched her retreat to take up a position behind the boulder, out of sight. He worried about the distance for a minute or two, and then—for a change—wondered whether a sword so light could possibly stop a large and determined monster. It was all very well to smite its skull in order to try and reveal a small gem embedded therein, but quite another to kill it instantaneously. He told himself that there was no point in worrying, but this didn't stop him.

He turned his attention to the water, watching the treacly ripples wandering slowly away from the cascade and smoothing themselves out.

How on earth, he thought, did I ever get mixed up in all this? I'm a scholar, the son of an instrument-maker, not a wizard or a hero-prince. Why couldn't some other poor fool have catalogued King Rufus's mouldy old library?

Why me? he asked the empty air. Why me?

The empty air didn't answer.

It came to Ewan in a flash of insight that even in everyday life not all questions *have* answers.

{13}

SIRION HILVERSUN STRODE into the council chamber of the palace at Jessamy. He wore the full regalia of his profession—a black silk cloak embroidered with every magical sign ever thought of, and a great pointed hat that made him seven feet tall. He also wore an expression which would have made the brightest day seem decidedly stormy.

As it happened, the only person in the council chamber was Prince Damian, who was wrestling unsuccessfully with a crossword puzzle. (Bellegrande was still away "seeking foreign aid," Alcover had gone to one of the smaller states in the Western Empire, famous for its casinos, "to study modern financial theory," and Hallowbrand had gone to a food fair in Heliopolis. Coronado had a diplomatic headache.) Prince Damian could be forgiven for the terrible shock and sense of disaster that overwhelmed him when he glanced up from twenty-six down to be confronted by the wrathful wizard. He would have run away had he been able, but his legs had somehow acquired the texture of jelly. He quivered instead.

"You pusillanimous pestilence!" roared Sirion Hilversun. "What have you done with my daughter?"

Damian, who thought that "pusillanimous pestilence" must be an incantation designed to turn him into something horrid, could find no answer.

The roar, however—penetrating to the deepest corridors of the palace—attracted others to the council chamber. The first to arrive was the queen, who somehow failed to recognize the enchanter—an amazing feat, considering that appearances were, for once, in no way deceptive.

"What are you doing here?" demanded the queen, in her most imperious voice. "How did you get in?"

"By broomstick," snarled Sirion Hilversun.

"Oh," replied the queen, nonplussed.

Damian, meanwhile, was still quivering so hard that his teeth began to chatter. He clamped his jaws shut and tried to control himself.

Rufus Malagig IV threw back the door and entered, apparently ready to lose his temper, but he pulled himself up as soon as he saw the enchanter. He, at least, had no trouble in recognizing the visitor.

"Magister Hilversun!" he exclaimed, with false warmth. "This *is* a pleasant surprise."

He stepped forward to shake the enchanter by the hand, but was interrupted by Damian, who called out: "Watch it, dad! He's gone crazy, or something."

The king stopped, unsure whether he ought to clip the prince round the ear for outrageous rudeness (not to mention sloppiness of expression) or to try and placate the enchanter (who did, he now noticed, have a faint hint of madness in the gleam of his eyes). He hesitated. In the meantime, Coronado arrived, clutching his forehead melodramatically. In the end, the king could manage nothing more regal than: "Er . . . to what do we owe . . . er . . . er . . ."

Sirion Hilversun didn't wait for him to finish. "I have come," he said, in a voice whose steadiness suggested monumental self-control, "to find out what your son has been playing at, involving my daughter in the most powerful spell the world has ever known."

"Oh," said the king, weakly. "Has he really?"

Coronado, realizing that this was no time for headaches, stepped forward briskly. "Do I understand, magister," he asked, "that you have only just discovered what has been going on?"

"You niggardly nincompoop!" said the enchanter, with feeling. "Do you think for one moment that I would have *permitted* my daughter to tamper with the legacy of Jeahawn the Judge?"

"Ah!" said the king, expressively (although just what he was expressing, no one was quite sure).

"Don't stand there braying like a jackass!" shouted the enchanter. "I want an answer. *Where's my daughter?*"

"*I* don't know!" retorted the red-faced Rufus, who had *never* been referred to as a jackass within the precincts of his own palace before. (Not, at any rate, to his face.)

"Should we know?" asked Coronado, smoothly.

"She went to Ora Lamae," snarled the enchanter. "To make sure that *he*"—here his finger stabbed out at the quailing prince—"was playing the game properly. *He's* here. Where's *she?*"

"Ah!" said the king, again, too late to stifle the sound.

"Oh," said Prince Damian, somewhat crestfallen.

The queen, who had caught up by now with the tide of events, gathered the prince to her bosom and extended her protective arms around him, despite his attempts to wriggle free.

"I fear," said Coronado, in tones of deepest regret, "that Prince Damian hasn't been anywhere near Ora Lamae. And perhaps, before we lose ourselves once again in a storm of accusations, insults and exclamations, I could be permitted to make one or two pertinent observations. . . . Thank you.

"Firstly, the choice of the questions forming the last will and testament of your enchanter friend was your daughter's. We did not understand what was happening and we still do not.

"Secondly, we have no knowledge whatsoever of the circumstances of the young lady's disappearance. The prince's . . . ah . . . emissary, sent out yesterday to fulfil the second demand, relating to the lamia in the Forbidden City, has not yet returned. As it is now rather late we had begun to fear that he never will return. If anything has happened to him—and, for that matter, to your daughter—then I would respectfully suggest that the fault lies not with us, but entirely with your daughter."

The enchanter moved his extended index finger so that it now pointed at Coronado. For a second or two, he hesitated between blasting Coronado from the face of the Earth and trying to figure out this whole bewildering affair. A second or two was enough to tip the balance in favour of the latter alternative. Coronado, not fully realizing how close he had come to extinction, swallowed hard.

"Who disenchanted Methwold forest?" asked the enchanter, his voice now level.

"Ewan," said Coronado.

"The prince's . . . substitute?"

"Yes," the prime minister confirmed.

"And he went to Ora Lamae? And hasn't returned?"

"Quite," said the prime minister.

"None of this was your idea?"

"None."

"Why did you take *your* question from the will?"

Coronado shrugged. "Ewan was looking for the answer to the first question in the library. He found the document. *We* assumed that we were supposed to follow the whole thing through. What else could we think?"

Sirion Hilversun lowered his accusing finger. "None of this is chance," he murmured. "None of it. It was planned. Long, long ago. Even the loss of my memory was planned, so I couldn't interfere. I should have realized . . . I should have thought. . . ." He looked up, suddenly, at the ring of faces staring at him. In a voice that was low and quiet, he said: "Jeahawn Kambalba was my mother's brother. We're related by blood. His power . . . still exists within us. Helen, too."

"I see," said Rufus Malagig IV, who didn't see at all, but felt compelled to say something.

"We thought we were setting up a marriage," murmured Sirion Hilversun. "I thought to establish a future for Helen, no doubt you had your reasons, too. But we weren't. We were being manipulated. We were setting up a spell. A powerful spell."

"Actually," said Coronado. "It's more of a chapter of accidents, really."

"And who do you think governs accidents?" snapped the enchanter, but not very viciously.

Coronado shook his head in mute disbelief.

"Why?" asked the enchanter. "Why did you want the marriage?"

"We wanted to bring you back to Jessamy," confessed

the prime minister. "The kingdom is bankrupt. We needed your magic to save us."

The enchanter laughed out loud. There wasn't much humour in the laugh. "My magic! Save a kingdom! I'm all but helpless, you pack of fools. I'm finished. I couldn't save a kitchen garden."

"Oh," said the king, dully.

"It was all for nothing, then?" said the prince, fighting free at last from the maternal clutch.

"Not for nothing," said Sirion Hilversun. "For Jeahawn the Judge. For his legacy to the magic lands . . . the last of his spells." He stopped, and half a minute dragged by while no one could find anything to say. Then the enchanter roused himself again, and said: "Well, what do we do now?"

"What *can* we do now?" countered Coronado. "Apart from waiting and hoping?"

"I need your help," said the enchanter, flatly.

"What for?" The answer came not from Coronado but from the king.

"To save Helen. What else?"

"What do you want us to do?" asked the prime minister.

"Come with me."

"To the magic lands? To Ora Lamae?" Coronado queried.

"Yes."

"If I thought for one moment," said the prime minister, smoothly, "that there was any help we could offer, then I would offer it. But you must realize that we are only ordinary people, despite our titles. We know nothing of magic or spells or enchantment. We sympathize with your difficulties. But there isn't really anything *we* can do to help."

"What you mean," said the enchanter, "is that you no

longer think you stand to gain anything."

"I assure you..." Coronado began.

"What about the boy?" interrupted Sirion Hilversun. Turning to the king, he added: "It might be your son. It *should* be your son."

"But it *isn't*," Coronado intervened, quickly. "And that demonstrates, I think, how wise we were not to permit the prince to risk his life. Ewan's a good boy. ...I like the lad. But we have to look at this thing realistically. The probability is that he's dead. He volunteered for this task. No one forced him. In fact, I myself recommended very strongly that he shouldn't go to Ora Lamae. The king and I both wanted to end the matter, on the grounds that it was too dangerous. The fact that the boy hasn't returned merely serves to affirm that we were right. I don't believe that we have any further responsibility in this matter. Your daughter chose to play a very dangerous game, and tried to involve us as well. I see no reason why we should now offer to risk *our* lives because she may have placed herself in peril. It's only common sense that we should disengage ourselves from the matter entirely. I see no other reasonable course."

"Or to put it another way," said Sirion Hilversun, "you're a coward."

"Not at all," said Coronado, quite unworried by the accusation. "I'm a politician."

The enchanter turned his steady gaze upon Damian. "What about you?" he said. "This boy's a friend of yours, isn't he?"

"Not exactly a friend," said Damian. "Don't like him much, to tell you the truth. Too clever by half. Anyhow, I never wanted to marry your daughter."

The enchanter raised his lightning-spitting finger again,

but only used it for a gesture of pure contempt. He looked at the king, then. "Do you really think that your kingdom is worth saving?" he asked. "For him? And for *him?*" He pointed, in turn, at the prince and at the prime minister.

"I'll go with you," said the king, quietly.

Prince Damian went white, and Coronado all but reeled with the shock.

"Sire," said the prime minister, "I must advise you most strongly...."

"Shut up!" said the king. "It's nothing to do with you."

"But, Rufus!" protested the queen. "Think of...."

"I *am* thinking," said the king. "I'm thinking that I'm sick of politics and all this worthless chicanery. I'm thinking that it's *my* fault that the boy's out there. It may not have been my idea, but I'm the *king,* damn it, and it's *my* responsibility. To hell with advice! I'm going! If there are any horses left in Jessamy, fetch two. If not, fetch donkeys. But move! I mean *you!*"

Coronado gulped. It was not the prime minister's job to fetch horses (let alone donkeys) but this did not seem to be the right moment to point that out. Coronado moved.

The king extended a hand to Sirion Hilversun, who accepted it in a firm clasp. "Let's go, magister," he said.

"Yes, your majesty," said the enchanter, his eyes burning as brightly as they had in twenty years and more.

The sun crept nearer to the horizon and was met by a fanlike array of cirrus clouds, which turned pink in its evening glow. The sky up above seemed, by contrast, a much deeper and clearer blue. And somewhere above the western horizon, shining like a beacon, was a single evening star. The air was very still and heavy, and rather warm for the time of year. The sound of the waterfall seemed to Ewan strangely dull and muted—but it was, at least, a real and natural sound. The deadly silence of Ora Lamae was one oppression that he didn't have to tolerate while he waited.

Helen, meanwhile, was thinking about the lamia and her company of halflings. The snake-woman and her cohort, she realized, had been just as trapped by the enchantments which lay upon the Forbidden City as the people who went in mortal terror of them. The spells that formed the units of Jeahawn Kambalba's will were not so much destroying them as setting them free. Zemmoul, she believed, would be no exception. He would rise from the murky depths of his own cold prison in response to the ritual offering . . . and he would meet the edge of the magic sword. Perhaps, she thought, dragons and their kin wait all their lives for heroes to put an end to them. Perhaps, if the truth were known, that's why they behave so strangely in respect of hoards of gold and pretty girls, neither of which can hold any particular attractions for them.

It was an interesting thought.

The sun retired modestly behind the feathery fan of cloud, which was advancing on a high breeze to cloak the western sky with radiant pink light, as if a great flock of flamingos was flying there.

Ewan, staring at the black water, saw a change in the pattern of the slow ripples, which curved in their paths as if pushed slightly askew by a swell that was rising in the centre of the pool. And, very quickly—or so it seemed—the water ceased to ripple at all but merely shimmered. Then it began to roll and to bubble, as though it were being *stirred* from within.

A thin black miasma began to rise from the surface and there was suddenly a stench in the air—an odour as if of something salty and slimy, ancient and rubbery. The surface of the pool boiled up like milk left too long on a stove, foaming copiously—but foaming black and not milky white.

These changes in the surface happened so swiftly that Ewan expected Zemmoul to erupt from the foam instantly, but he did not. Seconds dragged by . . . long seconds . . . while the black water churned and its black spindrift oozed over the bank of the pond and slithered over the grey mud and green moss around the weathered post.

Ewan stayed perfectly still, not daring even to shudder as the black stuff poured around his boots and clung to the fabric of his trousers. He wanted to call—or whisper, at least—to Helen, but terror froze his voice and left him quite helpless. He could do nothing but watch.

Then the foamy mass split asunder as Zemmoul's head burst into the warm air, turning from side to side and shaking off great gobs of viscous black oil. But still the head was covered with a glistening sticky sheen of the stuff, which clung to the flesh like an outer skin. At first, Ewan could see nothing of the monster's features but the shape of the vast bulbous skull which bobbed on the end of a thick rubbery neck which rose from the pool . . . and kept rising.

The head was the size of a haycart and the neck was as thick as a country road is wide. How long it might be he could not guess, and never would, for more and more of it emerged from the foam, and there was no end to it. Ewan thought briefly that Zemmoul might be a mighty serpent, but quickly realized that a serpent could not support itself thus, and that the monster's body must in actuality be so vast and cumbersome that it could never escape from the cavernous depths beneath the black pool.

Only the head and neck could ever reach out into the upper world.

Ewan watched the head go up and up into the sky, until it loomed above him like a tall tower. The neck could not hold rigid, and slow spiral waves passed up it, while the head, held aloft, moved in slow circles. Even as it attained the limits of its reach the head remained a half-shaped lump dressed in thick black slime ... but as it circled the sheath of slime *opened*— and there appeared an eye.

It was huge and round, with a glistening white ring surrounding a red circle with a vertical slit-pupil. The head dipped while the eye focused and began to scan the ground around the pool. There was only one eye, centrally placed in the skull.

Hardly had the scanning begun when it stopped. The head remained perfectly still for a moment or two, looking down.

Zemmoul had seen Ewan.

Then, without more than due pause, the gigantic head began to descend again, the neck looping sinuously.

Zemmoul did not snatch at his intended prey, but let his head down slowly and carefully. When it was halfway down the black sheath split again, as the mouth gaped wide, rimmed with a thousand gleaming teeth, each one a copper-colored dagger as long as a man's forefinger. Behind the teeth was a cavernous red maw, and flickering within it not one but a whole host of forked tongues— some yellow, some green, some blue and some creamy white.

The open eye, which was set directly over the upper lip, was staring straight at Ewan. The boy, curiously calm despite his terror, noted that above the eye was a rounded bump. There, he thought, is the setting of the gem.

And the heak kept coming down. . . .

And down. . . .

The jaws yawned wide to take him in, to catch him up and impale him with countless deadly needles.

A mere four or five feet above Ewan's upturned face the head paused momentarily. In that moment Ewan felt the disgusting breath of the monster envelop him, and as he breathed it in himself he felt a dark dizziness welling up in his brain. The breath was foul, but it was also sickly and hot, and it sucked at his consciousness like a powerful anaesthetic.

Time seemed to Ewan to freeze, and though he knew that the head was merely steadying itself for the final grab, not really hesitating at all, it seemed to him that everything was suddenly stilled . . . sealed within a single instant that might last for ever. . . .

Then the sword cut a glittering arc across his field of vision, and the edge of the blade, carried by all the force of Helen's overhead swing, cut deep into the black filth which clung still to Zemmoul's forehead.

The slime parted, and the skin beneath was sliced clean through. Then the blade met resistance and was turned aside, carving out a great mass of thick plastic flesh.

Revealed beneath was a jewel, shaped like a water droplet, whose colour was the deep, rich blue of the pure evening sky.

The monster snatched back its jaws, and the long neck rippled as it recoiled like a whiplash. Up and up into the sky, carried by a horrid convulsive reflex, went the bulbous head. And when the shudder had taken it as far as it would go, there was a single dreadful *crack* as the spine snapped and the bones were sheared.

Something like a water drop was hurled clear as the head began to tumble, the flaccid broken neck no longer able to support it. Seconds passed before the mass of flesh and bone crashed into the cascade, and more seconds while it was held by the white wall of water, tossed and buffeted.

In those seconds Ewan and Helen saw the black ooze washed away from the monster's skin and saw, for a few uncertain moments, the millions of tiny scales that were all the colours of the rainbow. But even as it was revealed the skin began to splinter and shatter, so that every scale fell separate and free. While they fell, like a glitter of hail in the spray of the falls, they became tiny living fishes.

The water in the pool never ceased to boil and bubble, but now the boiling and the bubbling brought countless gleaming silvery shapes to the surface. There must have been millions, catching the roseate light of the cloudy evening as they tossed and tumbled and were carried relentlessly over the lip of the pool, so that the stream which wound its way across the lands of World's Edge was alive with fishes.

Somehow the black ooze which had beset the pool and its outflow for centuries began, finally, to dissolve. The water did not become clear at once—nor could it, for the ooze was incalculably deep—but for the first time the great clear cascade began to have an effect. Hours hence—perhaps before the night was through—the blackness would have lost its dominance, and in a day or two there would be nothing of it left.

In the meantime, the dead hulk of Zemmoul, whose home the mud had been, was turning into fishes.

Ewan kicked off the broken shackle and rose slowly to his feet. Helen reached down to pick up the blue jewel which had fallen on the ground and was now exposed by the retreat of the black foam. She weighed it in her hand, and then started with surprise as it began to wriggle. She threw it back into the water, and it swam away, its vivid blueness lost immediately amid the multitude.

"Too bad," said Ewan. "It was pretty."

Helen shrugged. "I can conjure jewels out of pebbles any time," she said. "But conjuring fish is something else. It takes a special talent."

"I suppose it would," agreed Ewan.

"Well," said Helen, "that's the second stanza done. Two down and one to go."

"Another twenty-four hours like the last is going to be pretty heavy on the nerves," Ewan commented. *"My* nerves, anyhow."

"I don't think we have twenty-four hours," said Helen, bleakly. "I'll be surprised if we have more than four. I think we'd better start out for the Edge right now. The deadline for spells is always midnight."

The sun was gone, now, and the darkness gathering.

"I guess we can expect another visit from Wynkyn," said Ewan.

"Just as soon as it gets dark enough," agreed Helen.

She tied the sword to the mare's saddle-horn, and Ewan helped her up on to the animal's back. Then he mounted up himself.

"One thing," said Ewan, patting the grey mare's neck. *"She* seems to take it all in her stride."

"If we had her courage," said Helen, "I don't think we'd have to worry at all."

Then they rode off, towards the darkness that was descending from the east.

⊰(14)⊱

ALSO WATCHING THE gathering darkness were Sirion Hilversun and Rufus Malagig IV. They were in the great plaza of Ora Lamae, surrounded by a vast circle of shattered pillars, which had once been the world's finest colonnade but which now resembled nothing so much as a row of damaged teeth.

"Are you sure this is safe?" asked the king.

"Perfectly," the enchanter assured him. "There's no more magic here than in the courtyard of your palace. It's *gone*. Which means that Helen didn't fall prey to the lamia. Which may even mean...."

"Go on," prompted Rufus Malagig, as the enchanter hesitated.

"They're at least halfway through the spell," said Sirion Hilversun, slowly. "The thing is still working itself out. They may be already at Fiora . . . and if they survive their encounter with Zemmoul ... it's building up."

"I don't understand," complained the king, who was saddlesore, and no longer so sure that he had done the right thing in allowing the enchanter to bring him to this dreadful place.

"The last will and testament of Jeahawn the Judge," said the enchanter dully. "A spell to change the face of the Earth—to wipe it clean of the scars left by the wars. Helen and the boy are just its pawns, its instruments."

"Can we stop it?"

"Stop it! Two old men with two horses you borrowed from the local stagecoach, bones that ache and hardly enough energy to wipe the dust from our eyes? Stop it! If I were at the height of my power and you were Emperor of the West we couldn't stop it. Even Jeahawn Kambalba couldn't stop it now. He's wound this enchantment into the very cloth of existence—woven it into the pattern of history. As sure as the sun will rise tomorrow this thing will go to its destined end ... or, to put it another way, if it *doesn't* go through to its destined end the sun very likely *won't* rise tomorrow. Or ever again."

This statement, pronounced in tones as sober and intense as any that Rufus Malagig had ever heard, sent a chill into the king's bones. He had not enough imagination to allow for any real comprehension of what was going on, but he knew that if Sirion Hilversun thought that tomorrow's sunrise was in doubt, then it was, indeed, in doubt.

"I only wanted to save the kingdom," he murmured.

"Our motives were controlled just like our actions," said the enchanter.

"That's impossible!" protested the king, as a spark of his old self was ignited.

Sirion Hilversun didn't deign to reply.

"Then we're helpless," said the king.

"No," replied the enchanter. "We're not. We can't stop what's started, but we can co-operate. We can find a role *within* the pattern. We have to discover what kind of part we're *permitted* to play in all this. We may yet find that there's a way to save them . . . after they've done what's required of them."

"And how do we find out just what we can do and what we can't?" asked Rufus Malagig IV.

"That's simple enough," said the enchanter. "As soon as I get home I'm going to call up the shade of Jeahawn the Judge, and I'm going to ask him."

Wynkyn appeared while Ewan and Helen were passing through a small wood, which had once been inhabited by dryads and elves but which was now abandoned to the badgers and the voles. He drifted high among the branches and had his usual difficulty getting himself into focus.

"Play fair, now," he said. "Put out that lantern, please."

Ewan opened the lantern-glass and blew out the flame. Wynkyn quickly found his shape but ended halfway up a tree, sitting on a bough which certainly would not have borne his weight had he been substantial.

"You did a good job there," said the poet, to both of them, and then, looking at Ewan, added: "I'll forget what you said about my sonnets and assume you were affected by the strain."

"I didn't say anything about your sonnets," murmured Ewan. "I couldn't even find words to describe them."

Ghosts cannot, by their very nature, give people dark looks, but Wynkyn certainly tried.

"I'm afraid I'll have to take back the sword," he said. Helen untied it and held it out to him. He could not touch it, but he passed his hand close to it, and it rapidly lost its mass and disappeared.

"What do we get this time?" asked Helen.

"No magic, I'm afraid," said the apparition, whose voice sounded genuinely regretful. "I wish I could help, but I can't—not in that way."

"What can you do?" asked Ewan.

"I can give you a little advice," answered Wynkyn. "Don't look down."

"Is that all?" said Ewan. *"Don't look down.* That's all we get?"

Wynkyn spread his hands in a gesture of helplessness. "It's all *I* can do. You *will* get help, though . . . when you most need it . . . *if* things go all right."

"What do you mean, *if?*" demanded Helen.

"I mean *if,*" said Wynkyn, impatiently. "This whole thing still has ifs, you know. It's not automatic. Why do you think humans are involved at all? Because broomsticks and golems wouldn't do, that's why. It's not enough for you to go through the motions—you have to provide the rest as well."

"And what's the rest?" asked Helen.

"Courage, fear . . . a little pain. Determination, effort . . . everything that goes into living. How can you succeed if there's no danger of failure? This spell hinges on your success, and because it's a very, very important spell, there are very, very grave dangers involved. You have every opportunity to fail . . . because you have to have in order to have every opportunity to succeed. There's provision in the will for you to survive . . . *if* everything goes well. And I can tell you that it's not just you two who are involved. Others have to recognize and take their opportunities, too. There's a *lot* of ifs, and you mustn't forget that. If you think fate is looking after you no matter what, you're wrong. All fate has guaranteed you is the *chances*. You see?"

Helen nodded.

Ewan, after a moment's hesitation, nodded too. "It makes a kind of sense," he said.

"Well," said Wynkyn, "I'll tell you one more thing. I think it's okay. The rumours seem to have been right, for once. The Vaults Beyond could be packing up forever. No more curses to administer, spells to execute, enchantments to supervise. No more forms or files. The whole lot is to be locked up, and we'll all go on to our respective eternal rewards, *if* . . . I think you know what I mean."

"We know," said Helen. "You mean *if.*"

"And I wish you good luck," said the poet. "I really do." His little goatee bobbed as he nodded his head for emphasis.

"Thanks," said Helen, soberly.

"Thanks," echoed Ewan. "And Wynkyn. . . ."

The apparition, who had already begun to fade out, brightened again momentarily.

"Yes?"

"*Synchronous Sonnets* is okay. And the library of Heliopolis will look after it for a thousand years, *if*. . . ."

Wynkyn beamed magnificently. Then he faded out.

"Well," said Helen. "That's that."

"It certainly is," Ewan agreed. "How far do we have to go?" While he spoke, he lit the candle again, shielding the flame against the cool breeze as it flickered.

"Just over the next hill," Helen told him. "Then we're in the eternal mists. And the world ends at the top of the next slope."

"At the University of Heliopolis," said Ewan, "they think the world is round."

"Who knows?" replied Helen. "This time tomorrow, it might be."

Rufus Malagig IV was now feeling twice as saddlesore as he had when they had stopped at Ora Lamae. He wished that they had borrowed the stagecoach as well as the horses.

"Why did we have to come back here?" he demanded of the enchanter. "Couldn't you have summoned up the ghost in Ora Lamae?"

"No," said Sirion Hilversun, briefly. He was busy making preparations and didn't want to stop for long discussions. Actually, the reason that they had returned to Moonmansion was quite simple. Sirion Hilversun, in himself, could no longer lay claim to any significant magical power. But Moonmansion was positively saturated with magicality. There was magic in the stone walls and the captive air, and in the greatest collection of magical bric-à-brac surviving anywhere in the world. There were whole grimoires full of unused spells which still retained their own inherent power and needed no injection from their user. They were, for the most part, eccentric and peculiar spells that even an enchanter's lifetime would never find a use for, but there were still some good ones lurking among the junk.

The enchanter had brought the king down into the cellars, where the debris had accumulated even more obviously than everywhere else. There were boxes of books and trunks full of clothes, and crockery and furniture, and astrolabes and wallcharts, portraits whose eyes moved and skeletons which didn't, stuffed crocodiles and petrified plants, and jars and jars and jars—some with labels, most without.

Sirion Hilversun now stood in a space that was rel-

atively clear, sweeping away the dust from the floor with
a decidedly unmagical broom. The king, meanwhile,
moved some stained flasks and a distillation apparatus
from an ancient piano stool, and seated himself gingerly.
The piano stool groaned faintly, but this may have been
due to natural causes.

When Sirion Hilversun had brushed away the dust,
he began rushing round the room, peering at shelves and
dipping into tea-chests, periodically pausing to consult
a massive book he had brought from another room. He
gathered wands and bells and pieces of parchment. He
drew pentagrams on the floor, prepared candles of many
colours which burned with eccentric flames, mixed pow-
ders from dust-darkened jars with potions from glass-
stoppered bottles, and generally made ready to receive
his august visitor with all due ceremony.

The king of Caramorn, sitting on his stool and watching nervously, felt less like a mighty monarch and ruler
of men than he had ever felt before.

"It's very complicated, isn't it?" he ventured, when
the silence seemed intolerable.

"It's mostly for show," muttered Sirion Hilversun.
"Magic is a very showy art. I don't know why, but if
you don't go in for all the gaudiness and staginess it
doesn't work too well. All the best enchanters have been
hams."

"Are you *sure* you couldn't save my kingdom?" asked
Rufus, regretfully. "With *all* of this at your disposal?"

The enchanter snorted. "It's not only the process that's
mostly for show," he said. "Most of the effects are showy,
too. Omens and oracles and interviews with the extinct
are fairly straightforward, and you can conjure little things
to do extraordinary work for you. But saving kingdoms
. . . that's something else again. Your ancestor did more

than banish enchanters, you know. He banished the magic from the land itself. *That* made the difference. Most magical trickery has few enough lasting effects, and they're mostly bad. It's a great deal easier to put a curse on than lift one off, if you see my meaning."

The king sighed, not really following the argument, but knowing that the answer to his question was negative.

"Quiet, now," warned the enchanter. "I'm beginning."

With a wand in his left hand and a tiny silver bell in his right, Sirion Hilversun began to read from the pages of the great book. From time to time he paused to refer to a parchment that was on a lectern to his right, prevented from rolling up by two crystal paperweights which had once been eyes peering into eternity from odd angles.

Rufus Malagig watched the candle-flames dance and flutter to the rhythm of the spell, watched their coloured smoke curl and whirl with every insistent note of the little bell. He watched the walls seem to withdraw until they had hidden themselves in a pale smoky murk, and the ragged circle of piled-up junk become vague and unobtrusive, until they no longer seemed to be in the cellars of Moonmansion at all, but in some strange half-place beyond the known world, suspended between reality and illusion.

Rufus Malagig felt inside himself a dread so cold and alien that he wondered whether he, too, might not follow the hard rock into dissolution and half-existence. He was not really a brave man, and this dread gripped him wholly, eating away inside him. But he controlled himself, telling himself that once he had lived through this he need never be afraid again. Cold sweat formed in his eyebrows, but he would not even shiver.

Locked in this little spell-conjured bubble, out of phase

with all the manifold worlds, bounded and defined by the tiny candle-flames, the incantation came swiftly to its climax, and Jeahawn Kambalba appeared.

He was an old, old man—far more ancient in appearance than Sirion Hilversun, with his skin all but petrified and his whole frame consumed with an attitude of antiquity. His purple eyes seemed very large because they had no whites, but the purple was pale and weak.

The king had expected a taller man, a man still radiant with an aura of unearthly power, garbed as a fearful wizard in full panoply. But Jeahawn Kambalba was a small man, and he was wearing an old grey cloak without any markings, drawn in at the waist by a hempen rope. He was also round-shouldered.

For some seconds, he stood within his pentagram, staring at Sirion Hilversun. Then he said: "The call is answered."

"My name . . ." began Sirion Hilversun.

"I know your name. I know all names. Be quick. The names will not long hold power."

"My daughter," said Sirion Hilversun. "She is caught in your web. With a boy. We want to help them."

"There can be no help," said Jeahawn the Judge, quietly. "Not while they stand alone in Hamur and Sheal."

"And afterwards?"

"It is the end."

"Of what?"

"Of the ancient magic. Of the curses and the spells that have sickened the land beyond repair. Of the pestilence. Of the Abyss and of Chaos so close to Earth. Of everything that remains of Elfspin and Jargold, Viranian and Ambrael, of their wars . . . and even of the Age of Glorious Enchantment which was before."

"The end of this world," said Sirion Hilversun.

"The world always survives," said Jeahawn Kambalba. "But it is not always the same world."

"When the web is finished," asked Sirion Hilversun, "may we then help Helen and the boy?"

"Not with magic," replied Jeahawn.

"But we *can* help?"

"The cliff will crumble," answered the dead man. "The gates will break. The land will split and slip and slide. Black fires will burn and black floods quench them. Chaos will retreat, and the sea will come to claim it all. The sea will have everything. If they shall be saved, it is from the sea that you must save them."

There was a moment's silence when the shade had finished. While Sirion Hilversun hesitated, the image within the pentagram began to dwindle and fade.

"Wait!" called the enchanter, finding his voice again. *"When!* I must know *when!"*

The image was gone, the candles spluttering in a sudden cold, damp wind. But a voice came back . . . a voice out of nowhere.

"There are no more tomorrows, my sister's son. . . . There is only *now*."

{15}

WHEN THE MIST swirled around them, cutting off the starlight, Ewan's candle flickered and died. Helen frowned, because it was only recently that she had worked a spell that should have kept it alight all night. She recited the spell again. It did not work.

Ewan tried to strike a match to relight it in the normal way, but that wouldn't work either. Magic and logic were, it seemed, equally helpless here.

"It's because we're so close to Chaos," said Helen. "I've never been into the eternal mists before."

"How do we find our way?" asked Ewan.

Helen shrugged. "It's not far," she said. "And I think the mist has a faint light of its own. We'll get there."

And so they went on.

The mist which had shrouded the edge of the world since the dawn of time *did* have a curious light of its own, by which Helen and Ewan could see one another, but they could not see the ground on which the old grey mare walked. Ewan simply let her hold her own course. She seemed quite undismayed.

The air around them seemed to sparkle because of the illumination in the mist. It was almost as if they were walking on the bottom of an ocean bed, with tiny ripples in the water catching the sunlight from beyond the watery horizon. The light was an ochreous yellow in colour.

At first, there were trees and bushes beside the path that they followed, whose branches, white and frosted, intruded into their sphere of vision. But soon there were no more branches, and no more intrusions. There was only the mist.

"I don't like it," said Ewan. "I'm going to get down and lead her. I can feel the way with my feet."

He dismounted and knelt down to look at the ground beneath the mist. No grass grew here—there was just bare rock and ochre sand. The sand sat in the cracks in the rock, undisturbed by any wind. It seemed as if no wind had *ever* blown here.

Ewan stood up, dusting a little of the sand from his hand, where it had clung when he had touched the ground. The friction reminded him that his hands were still sore. They went on, Ewan leading the mare. He didn't feel apprehensive about their direction. It was as though it was built into him. He felt that he *couldn't* go wrong, and that while progress might be slow they were being drawn inevitably to their destination.

They didn't talk while they went on through the mist. Their doubts and uncertainties were crushed somewhere inside of them, and no longer could be voiced. Ewan did not look back to smile at Helen or to make any other gesture of reassurance. Though they were still together they each felt that in the mist they were essentially alone. The mist separated and isolated their minds, even though their bodies almost touched.

The coldness made Ewan's blistered hands ache somewhat, but it was a *clean* pain that he could easily ignore. His mind seemed unusually remote from the feelings of his body. His legs worked mechanically, and he was hardly aware of the measure of his stride or the fall of his feet. He could not sense the beating of his heart. Helen, too, was detached from the fatigue that afflicted her body. They were hardly aware of the passing of time ... if, indeed, any time was passing at all in the eternal mists.

Eventually, though, the mist began to thin out. The air was slowly drained of its yellow light, and they came once more into a clear night. The only difference was that here there were no shining stars: only an endless curtain of perfect darkness. There was light, but it was the strangest light they had ever seen. There were red flames, the colour of blood, drifting in the air—not high in the sky but near to them ... so near that Ewan might have reached out his hands and touched them as they drifted by ... flames where there was nothing to burn; cold flames. Ewan did not reach out to touch, afraid of what might happen to his hands if they made contact with such alien things.

Before them was a shallow upward slope of ebony rock, rough and cracked, but shining here and there with the reflected light of the flames.

Ewan glanced at Helen. She shrugged her shoulders. He understood what she meant. There was no further need to be surprised. The world they were in now had no responsibilities at all to expectations shaped by the one they had left on the other side of the mists.

Helen dismounted too, now, and they went on up the slope on foot, the grey mare plodding loyally after them. Helen and Ewan placed their feet carefully, afraid of the jagged rock. The only sound in this whole world was the ringing of the mare's metal shoes on the brittle black stone.

When they reached the rim, they could look out into chaos.

They stood on the edge of a vast, sheer cliff which fell away for ever beneath their feet. Far, far below there was a greyness that looked a little like an ocean and a little like a fog. But it was neither liquid nor gas, and it certainly was not solid—it was no material state at all, but something formless, that defied the eye to make sense of its aspect.

To Ewan, who had watched the surface of the black pool while Zemmoul had risen from the deep, it did not seem so terrible. The fear that stirred in his mind was a special fear, unlike any feeling that had ever woken there before. This was not merely the unknown, but the unknowable, something that human senses had never been intended to encounter, something the human mind was not equipped to cope with. He was not frightened so much as *dislocated,* his mind threatened not by any active or persuasive force but by sheer meaninglessness. The challenge was not to his courage but to his sense of being, his awareness of himself.

An uneasy vertigo, which sent slow, sullen waves of dizziness up his spine, made him step back a little way from the edge. He shook his head and shivered.

With Helen, the feeling was exactly the same. Though she had lived all her life in the magic lands, and was familiar with virtually all common supernatural creatures and manifestations, she, too, had no experience which had prepared her to cope with this. It was as completely alien to her as it was to Ewan. But she stood perfectly still, fighting very hard to stay outwardly calm. She knew that the worst was still to come.

Extending from the rim of the black cliff, forty or fifty yards to the left of where they stood, was a pair of narrow bridges. They started together but diverged at an acute angle. Each bridge was perhaps half a mile in length, and each one ended at the lip of an inverted cone of rock, suspended in mid-air high above chaos. On the flat, round top of each inverted cone was an archway— a simple flat-topped gate. Each bridge was about eight inches wide and seemed, at this distance, to have hardly any thickness at all.

Helen began to walk towards the point at which the bridges met the cliff. Ewan followed her. The grey mare followed Ewan.

They did not speak until they reached the starting point. Then, while they paused and contemplated the last part of their mission, Ewan murmured: "Don't look down."

"What?" asked Helen.

"Wynkyn's advice," said Ewan, raising his voice slightly. "Don't look down."

Human voices sounded eerie in this alien air, although Ewan could not quite decide what it was about them that was different.

"We've looked down," said Helen. "How could we help it?"

"I think it's while we're walking that we shouldn't look down," said Ewan. "Keep our eyes and our minds on the gates. Keep order in our thoughts. It wouldn't be wise to look into chaos while trying to balance on an eight-inch span that's no thicker than cardboard."

"True," admitted Helen.

"Self-composure is the key," said Ewan. "It must be. We have to keep our heads."

All this was obvious, but Helen let him say it all out loud. It was good to be able to talk, to make sense of it in words, to affirm some kind of determination and capability.

"Half a mile isn't far," she said. "It only takes ten minutes. Eight inches is quite enough. And the bridges will bear our weight. They must. We have to have a chance of getting there, or the whole thing's ridiculous."

"They'll bear our weight," agreed Ewan. "Perhaps that's why the spell selected us: we're neither of us very heavy. Seven-stone weaklings to save the world. Well, eight and a half."

"We're neither of us weaklings," murmured Helen.

"No," said Ewan.

There was a pause. Then Ewan said: "We'd better go."

And Helen said: "Yes."

And they went.

Walking the bridges was a battle between knowledge and imagination. Ewan *knew* that eight inches was quite wide enough to walk on without undue danger of falling off. He *knew*, too, that the bridge must be able to support his weight. And he didn't look down, because he *knew* that the abyss beneath him was irrelevant to the task in hand.

But knowing something is not the same as accepting it. In the apprehensive eye of his mind Ewan could visualize a false step that would topple him from the narrow black strip. He could visualize the ribbon of rock crumbling or cracking or dissolving into dust. And while he could not visualize the chaos that lurked below, he could certainly imagine all the sensations of falling . . . falling . . . falling . . . .

It took more than courage to walk the bridges. It took *conviction*—not the power of mind over matter but the power of mind over mind. Unlike the power of mind over matter, with which Helen was familiar, the power of mind over mind was something they both had to discover from first principles. But they did it, although they discovered in the process that half a mile is really a long, long way. They crossed the bridges.

Because the gates were slanted they could see one another as they took their stand within them. They were not directly facing one another, but they only had to turn their heads a little to meet one another's gaze.

The gates were not gates in the sense that they allowed access to some other world. They were just arches of rock. But as Ewan and Helen stood within them, shadowed from the glow of the drifting red flames, they each felt a sense of immanence, as though they genuinely did stand at the threshold not of two worlds but a thousand or a million—as though the whole of creation was close at hand. Perhaps, for those who knew *how* to use the gates, this nearness was actual, so that a traveller could step from the shadow to any place that is, was, or ever could be. But for Ewan and Helen, it was only a sensation—just a *feeling*.

Ewan, who stood within the gate named Hamur, experienced the feeling as a strange chill which seemed to begin deep inside his belly and slowly radiated outwards, consuming his entrails and running like quicksilver along his nerves to the tips of his fingers and his toes. Last of all it crept around the loculus of his skull, cradling his brain.

He didn't shiver.

Helen, who stood within the gate named Sheal, felt a numbness which grew from the back of her neck and oozed through her head and spine and extended a strange *stickiness* into all her senses, so that everything outside her became soft and heavy and grey and sweet, and she seemed within herself to become liquid.

She did not faint or sway.

It was Ewan who had to speak first, to keep the order of the spell, but Helen, her voice thick and slow, voiced the question for him:

> If you take your stand in Hamur's place
> at edge of world and gate of space
> what feeling creeps within your bone?

And Ewan answered: "Cold."

There was a pause. Then Ewan recited the second part of the stanza, prompting Helen:

> Aloof from Sheal the shadowed deep
> at edge of world and gate of sleep
> what do you feel as you stand alone?

And Helen replied: "Tired."

Then the world fell apart.

The black cliff crumbled into slick black sand. The cones of rock on which the gates stood began to melt, great gobs dripping into the abyss. The bridges shimmered and shattered and were gone, falling like tiny showers of metallic rain. As the gates themselves lost their shape and substance Ewan and Helen found their nightmare come true.

They fell.

But they did not fall like normal, solid objects. They fell like dead leaves or fragments of thistledown, borne up by an invisible force which might have been in the air that cushioned them or within themselves. They could not tell, and in their frightened minds it did not seem to matter, for the truth of it was that they were falling ... falling ... falling towards the grey chaos, and the horror of the feeling that came with the realization eclipsed all else within their minds.

Ewan wanted to stretch out his arms and put his legs together, to pretend that he could glide, but he couldn't make his brain control his body. It made no difference. Still he floated down.

Helen tried desperately to think of a spell—any spell that might offer any help at all—but no spell would come ... no rhyme at all.

The sky above them was no longer the even velvet blackness they had first seen on coming out of the eternal mists. It was turning grey and brown, and legions of blue-black boiling clouds were massing there. The red flames which had drifted in the air not far above them were ragged now, as if a dark, wayward wind was tearing at them, plucking them apart. Their light was fading now, but darkness did not come, because of the colour that was gathering in the sky. The last fragments of the black were slowly being banished, reduced to tattered banners which fluttered between the clouds and fell, flickering as they descended and looking for all the world like the ragged flames that were dying beneath them. It was as if the whole substance of the world was burning: red fire, black fire, blue fire ... all struggling to render the old reality into smoke and ashes.

Still Ewan and Helen were stranded in their nightmare, falling ... falling ... falling. ...

Then came the sound.

It was as if all the sounds that no one on Earth had ever heard were gathered together and joined into one *immense* sound which had no purpose other than to *make* itself heard, so that all the lost sounds of all the lost ages might make themselves meaningful at last, bursting upon human ears, to batter and scream and *live*, for a few fleeting moments, in human minds as a force . . . a terrible force . . . that mind could not resist. . . .

Ewan, twisting in the air, found the source of the sound far out where there should have been a horizon but somehow wasn't—where chaos curved to meet the dome of the black sky and somehow didn't. From out of that horizonless void, out of nowhere and nothing, a torrent of pale water was spewing. In moments, as his head turned and his eye saw, the water grew from a splash to a flood to a vast wall, already breaking into white surf at its crown, rushing out of nowhere towards the disintegrating land at incalculable speed.

Ewan spun then, so that he was no longer facing the onrushing tidal wave, but Helen saw it crash and tumble over the awesome face of chaos. She saw the incredible happen as the water was not absorbed into the chaos but the chaos into the water, so that the great grey ocean became an ocean in fact, in reality.

That frightful sound tearing at her ears was the triumphant cry of the flood and anguished dying scream of chaos.

Still they fell . . . but no longer into a limitless abyss where their bodies would evaporate and disintegrate. Now they fell toward the water, and they fell so slowly . . . so very slowly. . . .

Ewan felt the power of movement return to his limbs, and with one last glance at the burning sky he turned in his fall, stretched out his arms, and managed to hit the grey water almost vertically. It was no worse than diving from a ten-foot board.

Helen was not quite so fortunate—she twisted too hard and her limbs were still flailing as she hit the water. The impact knocked all the breath out of her, and while Ewan turned gracefully under water to bring himself back to the surface she floundered helplessly, unable to fight her way through the raging water to the air above.

As soon as Ewan's head was above the surface he gulped air and looked desperately around for Helen, but he could see nothing. A wave lifted him upon its crest, and he tried to look all around in the moment before it flung him down again, but still he saw nothing. Then he was submerged again, and fighting the water once more.

Helen, robbed of sight and feeling, with the water crushing her as she sank through it, got control of herself at last. She reached out with her arms and kicked with her legs, not upwards but sideways, until she was moving through the water like a fish. Only then, with her movements measured and definite, and her lungs desperate for air, did she turn in the water and go up like an arrow. It seemed to take a long, long time . . . and for a moment her mind—which seemed oddly remote from her body—contemplated the possibility that she might not make it in time. But then her head was free, and she sucked air into her lungs.

She tried hard to stay afloat, and looked for Ewan. But there was too much *wetness* oozing into her flesh. Released from the invisible hand which had cushioned her fall she was dropped into a world of brutal forces which still raged in conflict although the spell was now complete and the judgement of Jeahawn Kambalba brought to its conclusions. No magic could harm her now . . . but no magic could save her, and she was lost in a tempestuous sea. . . .

Somewhere there was a voice, calling her name. She knew it was Ewan, somewhere nearby, but she could not see him. The voice sounded fearful and forlorn. She tried to shout back, but salt water splashed in her mouth as she opened it, and she had to cough violently to get rid of it again. She tried to raise her arm as high as it would go, in case he could see.

The sea threw them together. It was pure chance, unaided by any guiding hand, but Helen felt her extended hand gripped suddenly, clasped tight and squeezed, and then Ewan was beside her in the trough of a great wave which immediately burst above their heads.

When they came up for air again, Ewan tried hard to speak.

"It's no use . . ." he began, and was stopped by the sea, which slapped him hard in the face. He had meant to say more, much more, but the waves would not give him the chance.

How far is the land? asked Helen, silently, of herself. What hope have we . . . if we have any hope at all?

She could not voice these questions, and so she let them die in her mind, concentrating all her effort in hanging on to Ewan. She looked up at the sky, which seemed no longer to be burning, but full of grey smoke and rain which fell all around them. Steep dark waves rose like hills on either side and she ducked her head before they could descend upon her, and did not lift it again until the impact was past.

Then, in a momentary calm, she saw something else in the water—something pale, more solid than the surf, that moved toward them. She tugged Ewan's arm, but he had seen it, too, and was already striking out in that direction.

"It's the horse!" yelled Ewan, close to her ear. "It's the mare!"

It was, indeed, the grey mare, helpless in the salt water and thrashing her forelegs in blind panic, but somehow coming ever nearer to them. Four or five strokes brought Ewan and Helen to her neck, and they released their grip on one another briefly as Ewan tangled his right hand in her mane and then tried to gain a similar grip for Helen.

"The neck," he gasped. "Put your weight on her neck. Try to balance her."

Somehow they got themselves into position, one on either side of the mare, each clinging tightly to her mane, forcing her forelegs down into the water lest her hooves tear at her own flesh. Thus stabilized, the mare could swim—and swim she did.

Together the three of them fought the waves, which were already beginning to lose their violence. Together, they survived.

Both Helen and Ewan knew, even if the mare did not, that their chances of survival were still very slim. If the tidal wave had inundated the magic lands and carried the flood to the borders of Caramorn—and both of them felt sure that it had—then they were a long, long way from any shore.

And what hope could there possibly be of rescue?

{16}

THE PEA-GREEN BOAT cut through the waves like a knife, bobbing as it rode the swell and dipping down the backside of each wave. The wind ran the tiny sail this way and that, and the vessel swayed drunkenly from side to side. But the water that splashed the deck never threatened to turn her over.

Sirion Hilversun spun the wheel and chortled with delight.

"Look at that!" he called. "No magic—no magic at all! Isn't she beautiful?"

Rufus Malagig IV, sprawled in the bows, had no idea what he was supposed to be looking at, and was far too sick to think *anything* was beautiful. He would have offered half his kingdom for just enough magic to keep the boat on an even keel. Not that half of his kingdom was worth a lot nowadays.

"It's getting clearer!" shouted Sirion Hilversun, either not knowing or not caring how much his companion was suffering. "We've ridden out the worst of it. If only they haven't drowned, we should be able to see them soon. The sky's getting lighter all the time. Look . . . it's almost blue now!"

Rufus Malagig tried to look up at the sky but was seized by such a terrible attack of nausea that it would have made no impression upon him if the sky had been pale puce. He groaned hollowly—a groan that would have done credit to any ghost.

It was still raining, but it was hardly more than a drizzle now. The waves were rapidly becoming calm. When they had launched the boat from the south-east tower as the tidal wave had crashed against the walls of Moonmansion it had been touch and go as to whether they would survive ten minutes. Without Jeahawn Kambalba's warning, they might have been trapped in one of the downstairs rooms, in which case they wouldn't have stood any chance at all. Now they were almost certainly safe themselves and were mounting a desperate search for Ewan and Helen.

Sirion Hilversun half turned to look at his companion and was horrified to see him sprawled out on the deck, with his head propped up against the bow rail.

"Get up, man!" he yelled. "I can't look every way at once. On your feet, damn you!"

Rufus Malagig IV felt that this was no way to speak to a king—especially not a seasick king—but he could not find sufficient strength to complain. He knew, though, that the situation was urgent, and that if he had any small reservoir of heroism left untapped, now was the time to tap it.

"Come on!" urged the enchanter, who was an enchanter no more.

The king forced his legs to move, and with great difficulty pulled himself up into a kneeling position. He put his hand up as if to shade his eyes (actually, he was holding his head, which felt as if it might drop off at any moment) and assumed an attitude of keen vigilance, looking out to starboard.

Satisfied, Sirion Hilversun directed his own gaze to port, although occasionally—not wishing to take too many chances—he sneaked a quick glance to starboard to make sure that Rufus Malagig wasn't missing anything.

The king, though, really was trying his hardest, fighting down the seasickness and scanning the waves anxiously for the least sign of anything hopeful. And he it was, in fact, who first caught sight of the white head bobbing in the water. For a moment, he could not see what it was and almost rejected it as a folly of the foam— an illusion sent by the waves to distract him. Then he saw the pale arms clinging to the mane, and the smaller, darker heads. He yelled wordlessly to Sirion Hilversun, jabbing with his outstretched arm.

The enchanter spun the wheel to bring the little boat about.

"Get the rope!" he called.

The king of Caramorn, babbling incoherently, scrambled across the deck to the foot of the mast and began to uncoil the rope secured there. Sirion Hilversun almost came to help him, but the moment he released the wheel it spun back and the boat lurched horribly, so that he had to return to steady it.

Rufus Malagig crawled away from the mast, the rope in his arms, and tried to stand. He looked dazed.

"Give me one end to tie down," said the enchanter desperately. "Throw the other end to them and haul them in."

The king came to his feet at last, staggered drunkenly, and seemed about to fall overboard. Then he gained belated possession of himself and tossed several coils of the rope to the old man, who promptly began winding the slack around the stem of the wheel, tying a knot every three or four loops. The king threw the rest of the rope over the side. It fell far short of the target. Without a moment's hesitation, Rufus Malagig IV dived over the side, grabbed the end of the rope, and began swimming hard towards the horse and the two clinging to its neck.

Ewan and Helen saw him coming and tried to reach out to help him. Ewan did not realize, at first, who it was, and was shocked when he heard the familiar voice gasping at him.

"Take the rope!" said the king, thrusting forward the free end. "Hang on—both of you. I'll swim back, pull you aboard."

Ewan took the rope and wrapped it swiftly about his wrist. With his other hand he took Helen's arm, and the two of them floated free of the mare. The king was already swimming back to the boat.

Sirion Hilversun looped the rest of the rope that was slack at his end through the spokes of the wheel, securing it firmly. Then he ran to the side in time to help Rufus Malagig back into the boat. As the king somehow contrived to ease his bulk up and over, sagging to the deck immediately, the enchanter heard him moan.

"Are you hurt?" asked Sirion Hilversun.

"No-o-o..." replied the king. "But I feel... *terrible!*"

Nevertheless, Rufus Malagig regained his feet, all his clothes clinging wetly to his body and his hair dripping salt water into his eyes. Both he and the enchanter grappled with the rope and began to haul upon it. Ewan and

Helen, quite exhausted, could do little enough to help them, but within minutes they were beside the boat, and arms were reaching down to help them over the side.

The moment they were in, and safe, *everyone* collapsed. All four of them lay in the scuppers, surprised and grateful that all they had to do, for a minute or two, was breathe.

The enchanter was the first to rouse himself, and he moved to take his daughter in his arms. He sat on the deck, cradling her head upon his lap for a long time. Rufus Malagig did nothing but pant and wonder why his nausea just wouldn't go away. Ewan managed to kneel, and he looked over the side. For a moment he didn't know what he was looking for, and when he remembered, he realized that it wasn't there. There was no sign at all of the old grey mare. Her head had finally vanished beneath the waves, and she had lost the unequal struggle.

"She saved us," murmured Ewan. "She saved us . . . and we couldn't save her."

Then he burst into tears and didn't stop, even when he felt Helen's hand upon his shoulder and heard a voice saying: "She was so old, there was no way . . . but we're safe. Safe now."

He just couldn't stop at all.

Much later, the little boat reached the shores of Caramorn. The water lapped gently against the side of a shallow hill, and they stepped out on to springy green grass. They were all quite recovered by now. Even Rufus Malagig felt as if he could quite confidently step back aboard and face the waves again. His stomach was quite settled, although he did feel rather hungry.

Sirion Hilversun looked out over the expanse of blue water, which sparkled in the morning sun.

"Gone," he murmured. "All gone. The lands where magic ruled. Moonmansion . . . everything. All under water. Finished. For ever."

"You realize what this means?" said Rufus Malagig IV.

"Oh, yes," said the enchanter. "I've lost everything. Everything except. . . ." He placed his arm protectively around Helen's shoulder. She too was staring out to sea, thinking about all that was gone for ever.

"Caramorn has a coast!" said the king, who sounded far from unhappy. "We can build a fishing fleet! We can build ports. This is a *new* ocean—unfished, unexplored. This will be the making of Caramorn. . . . The country's future is safe. No more depending on getting good harvests out of bad farmland! Don't you see . . . ?" He trailed off then, realizing that what had happened meant something very different to Sirion Hilversun and Helen. "Look," he said, quietly. "Don't take it so hard. Caramorn is your home, now. We still need you there."

"What for?" said Sirion Hilversun, bitterly. "I've no magic now. I can't remember tomorrow any more. Everything I had is drowned with Moonmansion. I'm just a useless old man."

"No," said the king, thinking quickly for once. "Not everything is gone. It's not *all* lost. You may not remember tomorrow, but you remember yesterday . . . a great many yesterdays. You've lived a long time—you know more than any other living man. And you have more than knowledge . . . you have wisdom. We need you at Jessamy. I want you to be one of my ministers. And there's something else, too. If you'll agree, I want you to become Damian's tutor. He's growing up, now—and someone has to help turn him into something resembling a king. There's a great deal he has to learn—and it won't be easy teaching him. I can't do it, and neither can the other ministers—they're just a bunch of petty politicians. Coronado will save the country all right, now that things are different, but someone has to save Damian. How about it?"

The ex-enchanter looked long and hard at the king. Finally, he said: "What about Helen?"

"I've already decided what I want to do," said Helen, quickly, just in case the king, carried away by his magnanimity, suggested that she marry Damian.

"What's that?" asked Sirion Hilversun.

"I'm going to Heliopolis," she said. "To the university. With Ewan."

Ewan looked up when he heard this declaration, and for the first time since Rufus Malagig had hauled him out of the sea, he smiled. It was a long, long smile.

The enchanter looked at the king again, dubiously.

"It's a good idea," said Rufus Malagig.

"Will the Treasury be able to stretch to two grants?" asked Ewan.

"We'll manage," said the king. "Somehow, we'll manage."

Sirion Hilversun shrugged his aged shoulders. "In that case," he said, "I suppose we'll all manage."

Then, with the sun on their backs, they all began the long walk home.

Fantasy from Ace
fanciful and fantastic!